Marcus

Mischa

Vargmannen

Ia

Gunilla

Three Cave Mountain

Three Cave

Mountain

OR: GRANDFATHER AND THE WOLVES

PER OLOV ENQUIST

Illustrated by Stina Wirsén

TRANSLATED FROM THE SWEDISH BY
TIINA NUNNALLY

THE OVERLOOK PRESS
WOODSTOCK & NEW YORK

This edition first published in the United States in 2007 by
The Overlook Press, Peter Mayer Publishers, Inc.
Woodstock & New York

WOODSTOCK:
One Overlook Drive
Woodstock, NY 12498
www.overlookpress.com
[for individual orders, bulk and special sales, contact our Woodstock office]

NEW YORK:
141 Wooster Street
New York, NY 10012

LONDON:
90-93 Cowcross Street
London, EC1M 6BF
inquiries@duckworth-publishers.co.uk
www.ducknet.co.uk

Translation assistance provided by the Swedish Institute

Cataloging-in-Publication Datais available from the Library of Congress

Book design and type formatting by Bernard Schleifer
Manufactured in the United States of America
ISBN-13 978-1-58567-913-3
10 9 8 7 6 5 4 3 2 1

For
Cecilia Enquist, Marcus Enquist, Mina Gilbertsson,
and Moa Gilbertsson, who were there and endured it
all. And for Karlstad Hospital, the Värmland Rescue
Service, and the Arvika police, with gratitude for
their superb efforts under difficult circumstances.

—P.O.E.

Contents

Three Cave Mountain

CHAPTER 1

A Horrible Night

1.

THIS IS HOW IT HAPPENED.

Afterwards Mina could hardly remember how it started. She said that she was so little back then, and she was scared. Since then she has almost never been scared. She didn't really know how it happened. Sometimes Grandpa would remind her. Then she would simply say:

"Well, that was in the past. I was so little back then."

Even though "in the past" was only three weeks earlier. It's strange how you can grow up in three weeks. And you can't really.

But this was how it all started.

Mina was six years old. She had blond hair and green eyes, and lots of boys in her school thought that she was very sweet, but she didn't pay any attention.

There was so much a person had to put up with, including love, as her mother, whose name was Jenny, had told her. But one night, just as Mina was falling asleep, a crocodile bit her on the behind.

That was the first time Mina was ever bitten by a crocodile, and she was only six. She woke up and could feel it hurting. At first she lay in bed, trying to figure out exactly how much it hurt, whether it hurt a huge amount or just a little, and whether she was going to have to roar like crazy so that Pappa and Mamma would come. She couldn't really make up her mind, but then she remembered how horrible it was when the green crocodile attacked and chomped on her behind. So she decided that it really was horrible, and she started to cry.

Then her Pappa, whose name was Anders, came into the room. He looked as if someone had dumped a plate of spaghetti on his head, and in a grumpy voice he said:

"What is it now? I need to sleep."

Then Mina sobbed for a little while longer, as if she were about to die or she had some awful illness that Pappa would have to cure instantly, for example by giving her a Popsicle or a hot dog with ketchup. But after she had cried for a while, she felt worn out and almost stopped, but kept on sobbing inconsolably. Almost as if she had been left all alone in the woods. And then she gave a deep sigh. Because Pappa simply sat on her bed and stared and was not at all alarmed.

Mina always liked it best when Pappa and Mamma were so alarmed that they practically exploded. Then they would go down to the freezer and get her some ice cream. Once when she was four, she started howling because she fell down and broke her leg. At least that's how it felt, she was almost positive, until finally Mamma picked up the phone and said that now, darn it all, she was going to call an ambulance. And then Mina was so happy that she stopped howling, just like that. She said she wanted to sit up front, next to the man driving the ambulance. But then Mamma put down the phone and said she knew darn well it was nothing after all. And it was lucky that she hadn't called the ambulance. But then Mina got mad and said that if Mamma kept cursing like that she'd have to wash out her mouth with soap, top to bottom and underneath her tongue too, and maybe even down her throat.

But then Mamma asked her how her broken leg felt now.

And Mina forgot which leg was broken, and she pointed to the wrong one. And then her mother started laughing and went to get her some ice cream.

If you want ice cream, you have to be very inventive.

The fact was that Mina was sure she had been attacked by a crocodile in the night. She remembered very clearly that she was on the bank of the awful Congo River, where the cannibals swam and sunbathed and slept on the beach in the sunshine after they had eaten their fill of each other. They ate each other's legs, and no one objected or thought it was strange to be eating each other. Although they only ate the legs. Everyone was nice. No one screamed or swore or washed their tongues with soap. And they ate the most from a very fat boy. He was nice and would spread ketchup on his legs whenever the little cannibals appeared, hungry for his legs.

They ate his legs with ketchup, but without mustard or bread. But then she remembered that she went down to the water of the Congo River to swim because she didn't feel like eating legs with ketchup. And that's when the crocodile appeared.

It was small and green, and she recognized it, because Pappa had an emblem on his shirt that looked just like that crocodile. Mina recognized the crocodile from Pappa's shirt, although now it was bigger, so it wasn't an exact copy, plus it was moving. And in a very stern voice, Mina said to it:

"Did you escape from Pappa's shirt? What kind of behavior is that? Swim back this instant or else Pappa's going to be really mad!"

But the crocodile just kept swimming around like crazy, glaring at Mina, and he said he didn't know what she was talking about. He told her he was a dangerous

crocodile swimming in the Congo River, and things like that, and she should watch out.

"Watch out yourself!" said Mina. "And swim right back to Pappa's shirt!"

"Watch your butt," said the crocodile, very mad. And then he jumped up and bit her on the butt.

That was how it happened. And then Mina woke up and it hurt where the crocodile had bitten her. And after thinking about it for a minute, she decided to howl like a stuck pig. I have to yell for help! she thought. It won't do any good to lie here and suffer in silence.

And so she started howling. Then Pappa came in, with his face all scrunched up, as if he hadn't gotten enough sleep.

"Your crocodile bit me," said Mina.

"What did you say?" asked Pappa.

"On the butt!" sobbed Mina. And she pointed.

And believe it or not, there was a gigantic lump. As big as a half-krona coin.

"That's a mosquito bite," said Pappa as he tried to smooth out his scrunched face. "It's just a mosquito bite. Nothing to be scared of. Go back to sleep now, sweet little Mina."

"It was a crocodile," roared Mina, louder than ever. "I saw it. It was green. A mosquito isn't green, is it? Or big like a crocodile!!!"

"Go to sleep, honey. Try to understand. I have to get some sleep. It's Sunday, honey," said Pappa, as he got up and was about to close the door.

"It bit me!"

"You were dreaming," said Pappa. "Go to sleep now. It's nothing."

"I know when I'm dreaming!" cried Mina. "And this is not something that I dreamed!"

"You're just imagining things," said Pappa. "You'd better stop that or you'll end up like Grandpa."

"I want to be like Grandpa," said Mina in a grumpy voice. "He would have protected me from the crocodile."

"No doubt," said Pappa. He was Danish, and people said things like "no doubt" in Denmark. "But you're going to wake up Moa!" said Pappa.

And then he went back to his bedroom and rolled into bed and probably fell asleep instantly.

Moa sat up in bed and stared at Mina.

"CROCODILE!" said Moa, and she looked wide awake. Moa wanted to have a crocodile that bites too!

Mina was really annoyed. "What a brat you are," she said. "You always have to have everything."

Mina knew that it wasn't a dream. Pappa was always sleepy and Mamma was asleep. Moa probably wanted to play now, but Mina didn't want to play at all.

This was urgent. Nobody took her seriously. And she thought that she'd really like to have someone who would rescue her whenever she was in trouble. It was important to have a Benefactor, as Grandpa always said. That was someone who always stood up for you, like whenever the grown-ups said "try and understand" and wanted to sleep. Or watch golf on TV.

And she thought that good advice was costly, as old Grandma Vega used to say. But Mina didn't have any money.

She was going to have to consult Grandpa. That was the answer. He was the only one who would understand how extremely serious the situation was.

And that was actually how it all started.

First there was the awful night with the crocodile. Then came the other events, and finally the almost fatal expedition up to Three Cave Mountain and what happened with the wolf cub.

CHAPTER 2

Grandpa Steps In

1.

AFTER MINA HAD THOUGHT THROUGH EVERYTHING, SHE decided to call Grandpa. He was bound to have an idea. He didn't have as much to do as everybody else, so he had more time to think up ideas.

She had to think through what had happened. It wasn't easy to understand.

The crocodile had escaped from Pappa's shirt and bit her on the butt, and she was a little scared. The crocodile that bit her in the night was much bigger than the emblem on Pappa's shirt; she clearly remembered that. Maybe crocodiles got big at night and shrank in the morning. The critter was on the loose at night. For a moment she wondered if she should wake up Pappa again to explain, but he would just get mad and start muttering. Instead she decided to go look in the refrigerator to see if there were any hot dogs, and there were.

* * *

It was Sunday, and first she looked at Pappa's shirt to see if the crocodile was still there. But it wasn't. There was no emblem on his shirt.

The crocodile was on the loose, and the lump on her behind was still there. It didn't hurt as much, but she checked in the mirror and she was almost positive that she could see teeth marks. That was proof that she hadn't just dreamed it all up.

Then she went down to the kitchen. After a while her little sister Moa came downstairs and said:

"I want a hot doggie, Ina!"

"Don't talk baby-talk!" said Mina sternly. "And besides, you shouldn't eat hot dogs this early in the morning."

The cat was sitting in the kitchen window. They had named her "Cuddles" because Mamma was hoping that she would be a nice, cuddly cat, but sometimes Cuddles

could be mean if she didn't get her food on time. Then she was definitely not cuddly. She'd say she was going out to catch baby birds if she didn't get some liver sausage. So Mina would give her liver sausage, and then Cuddles would be cuddly again. Mina often talked to Cuddles when they were alone, but not at any other time, because then Cuddles wouldn't answer.

Cuddles never said "try and understand."

"Cuddles," said Mina, "a crocodile came after me in the night, and bit me."

"So what am I supposed to do about it?" said Cuddles in a grumpy voice.

"I'm scared that she's going to come back tonight," said Mina.

"How do you know it's a girl crocodile?" said Cuddles.

"She was so grumpy and mad, and boy crocodiles aren't like that. At least that's what Pappa says."

"He doesn't know what he's talking about," said Cuddles. "I wouldn't mind a little liver sausage, by the way."

"You're getting fat," said Mina. "You shouldn't eat liver sausage." But then Cuddles got very grumpy and went looking for something else to eat.

Mina had nobody she could really talk to. What should she do? She had a cousin she always called on the phone. Her name was Ia, and Mina knew her phone number by heart. Ia lived in Bälinge. Mina decided to call

Grandpa first, but he didn't answer. He was probably out taking a walk with his dog, whose name was Mischa. So she called Ia. But Mina's uncle Mats answered the phone, and his voice sounded mad and grumpy.

"Do you know what time it is, Mina? It's only eight o'clock, and I'm terribly—TERRIBLY—tired and need to sleep. Do you HAVE to call so early?"

"Why are you so tired?" asked Mina. "I'm not tired at all, even though a crocodile bit me in the night."

"Honey," said Uncle Mats. "Honey. Try and understand. I'm totally done in and worn out, and honey, it's Sunday. Can't you—"

"But you weren't bitten by a crocodile!!!"

"Honey. Try and understand. I've got a pulled muscle in my calf and I have to play golf today. Try and understand. I NEED to get some sleep, and do you HAVE to—"

"I'm scared the crocodile will come back!" said Mina.

"Why don't you talk to Ia instead. But not now. Honey. I'm TERRIBLY tired and worn out and HONEY, don't call us so early next time."

"How early should I call next time?"

"Much later," said Uncle Mats, and hung up.

Mina sat down to think. It seemed hopeless. Mamma and Pappa were asleep, and Moa was playing a computer game. Even though she was only four, she was a whiz at computer games. Cuddles had managed to pry open the pantry door, but she couldn't open the refrigerator, so Mina didn't pay any attention. But who could she talk to?

2.

She waited an hour, which was how long it usually took Grandpa to walk Mischa in the morning, and then she called again. Grandpa answered the phone.

Mina's grandpa was a tall, handsome grandpa with white hair. He was always so nice, and he didn't have a lot to do because he mostly sat and wrote. He didn't have a real job. He just wrote books. But he never hung up when she called, and he always had fabulous advice to give, even though all the other grown-ups thought it was bad advice. And he could tell such great jokes about poop, and he liked to tell fart stories at the dinner table, and that was so much fun. But then Mina's mother would almost always get mad and take him by the arm and lead him out to the bathroom, so that the children would learn to behave themselves. And Grandpa would have to sit in there for an hour as punishment. Whenever Grandpa was locked in the bathroom for telling fart stories, nobody was allowed to talk to him. But Mina would fool her mother. She would sneak up to the bathroom door and whisper through the keyhole, telling her grandpa not to cry. And after a while Grandpa would stop crying because he was so happy that Mina felt sorry for him. Mina used to say "shh-shh" and "now now" through the keyhole in the bathroom door because that's what you say when someone feels bad. And then he would whisper a short, funny fart-and-poop story through the keyhole. But one time Mamma caught them and got really mad, and then she dragged Mina by the hair away from the door, and Grandpa had to stay in the bathroom almost all night long. Mina was almost sure she remembered the whole thing.

Grandpa was the sharpest and smartest person in the whole family, even though he didn't have a decent job and just wrote books. But not everyone realized this, except Mina, and maybe Moa, but she was so little. In any case, Moa couldn't understand what Cuddles said.

Grandpa had a dog named Mischa.

She was a smart, beautiful dog, and the children loved her even though she looked like a wolf. And she was a lot of trouble to everyone except Grandpa. He was the only one who ever took her for walks. And sometimes he would give her scraps of food at the table, even though he wasn't supposed to. Mischa was born on the Siberian tundra in

faraway Russia. Her mamma and pappa were sled dogs, and Mischa was seventeen years old. That meant that she was one hundred and nineteen in human years, and so she was even older than Grandpa. Mischa was big like a wolf and nice like an elephant, as Grandpa used to say. She lived in Waxholm with Grandpa and Gunilla. Sometimes, especially when Grandpa made a fool of himself and was locked in the bathroom, Mina would lie down on the floor and use Mischa as a pillow. She would whisper to the dog about how dumb everybody was except for Grandpa and Mischa. That was so cozy, but she could only do it when Grandpa came to visit.

Grandpa lived with Gunilla. They were married. She was nice and never locked Grandpa in the bathroom. She

was Grandpa's wife even though she was not Mina's grandmother. That's how things are sometimes! as Gunilla always said.

Grandpa had once told Mina that he had married Gunilla because she had such nice melons. So the next time Mina went to visit them, she looked at the melons growing in the yard, and then she told Gunilla: there's nothing special about your melons. And she couldn't understand why that was the reason Grandpa had married her. But Gunilla didn't know what she was talking about, and then she got a funny look on her face and said "Huh" in a strange way. So Mina again pointed at the melons growing in the yard and said that was the only reason Grandpa had married her. That's what he said. Then Gunilla said that Grandpa had a poetic nature and that's why he talked so much about nature, such as her melons, because that's what nature lovers do.

Grandpa had explained that Gunilla was a feminist, and that meant that Grandpa had to clean up after himself, and he was never allowed to ask if he could "help out" with the housework, because that was something he was expected to do without asking.

But sometimes Gunilla had a hard time understanding. For example, she didn't want to get another dog. Grandpa wanted to have a little dog to keep Mischa company, but Gunilla thought that would just cause even more trouble.

So that morning Mina called Grandpa and told him the whole story about the crocodile.

"Why, that's crazy," said Grandpa. "What about your miserable parents, what are they doing about it?"

"Nothing," said Mina. "Absolutely nothing. And Uncle Mats just wants to sleep."

"What did he say?" asked Grandpa.

"He said 'try and understand.' That's what he said. And that I shouldn't be waking him up."

"That's nuts," said Grandpa. "You need to find someone who can protect you."

"But who?" said Mina. "You just get locked up in the bathroom. And then they keep on saying 'try and under-

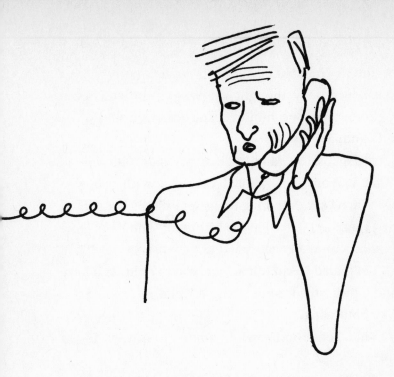

stand' all the time, and they want to sleep. You told me that
I should find a Benefactor whenever I'm in big trouble."

Grandpa was thinking so hard that his head creaked.

"The police," he said.

"There are hardly any police around anymore," said
Mina. "And you have Mischa to protect you. But I only
have Cuddles, and she's mad at me right now and doesn't
want to protect me."

"What you need is a Benefactor dog," said Grandpa.
"If you're attacked by crocodiles, you need to have a
Benefactor. Just the right little dog, for instance. Or
something else like that."

Mina thought about this for a moment. She knew

what trouble Grandpa had gone through to keep Mischa, because everybody thought she was so difficult, even though she was one hundred and nineteen and older than Grandpa.

"A dog," said Grandpa, "that will stay with you all the time as your Benefactor. I can't stay with you, you know. When I say the wrong thing, for example, or tell fart stories, then I get locked in the bathroom. And if the crocodile shows up then, well, good Lord, what can I do?"

"I'm scared," said Mina. "But you're right. You have to find a protector for me. I have a feeling."

"About what?"

"That something awful almost positively might happen."

"Unless," said Grandpa. "Unless."

Mina could hear in the phone that Grandpa was thinking so hard that his head was making that special creaking noise.

"You know what?" he said. "Tomorrow Gunilla and Mischa and Ia and Marcus and I are going out to the house in Värmland. For two weeks. Would you kids like to come along? Then we'll have time to plan. And maybe we can buy you a Benefactor dog who will protect you from the crocodiles. But above all . . . we'll make a plan to help you."

Mina closed her eyes and thought hard. Just imagine going to Värmland with her cousins! And Mischa would sit in the space behind the back seat. How fantastic it would be if Grandpa bought her a little Benefactor dog. Then they would have two protectors: both Mischa and a new little dog that Grandpa would buy and give to Mina without telling her parents about it.

"A plan?" said Mina.

"Actually two plans. First we'll get the Benefactor dog from the kennels in Västerås. It has to be a schnauzer and only three months old."

"And then?"

Grandpa was silent, thinking without saying a word.

"Do you really have two plans, Grandpa?" asked Mina in a whisper because she could hear Pappa and Mamma moving around in the kitchen. "Talk softly so they won't hear you, Grandpa!"

"Okay," he said. "I have a second plan too. But we have to keep it to ourselves. Don't tell anybody that we're going to buy a Benefactor dog. Not your mamma or your pappa or your uncle Mats, and maybe not even . . . no, maybe not. Maybe we shouldn't say anything to Gunilla."

"What's your second plan?" said Mina. "Spit it out, Grandpa. This isn't about your poetic nature, is it, Grandpa?"

"Nope," said Grandpa.

"Then spit it out!"

Grandpa took a deep breath. "Point A: We have to get you a dog as a protector. And we'll name her Elsa. But that's a long-term plan. More important is Point B. Point B: We have to go up to the house in Värmland to plan an expedition. If someone is nervous about crocodiles attacking again, she has to do something spectacular. Then an attack by crocodiles will just seem trivial. For instance, she go on an expedition. And everyone has to go along, everyone. She has to do something that will conquer her fear. *Comprende?*"

Sometimes Grandpa used strange words like that, but if you just nodded and pretended to understand, he was happy and kept talking.

"I know what the expedition should be," said Grandpa. "Up to Three Cave Mountain. Anyone who goes on that expedition will never be scared again. Not of anything."

"Is it dangerous?" asked Mina nervously.

"Not if you stay with the group. And if you go on that expedition, nothing will ever scare you again. Nothing."

"Not even a crocodile?"

"Especially not a crocodile."

"Are we going to expeditionize without Mamma and Pappa?"

"Uh-huh. Just us. And Ia and Marcus and Moa, but no one else."

"What about Gunilla?"

"Of course. That's what I said. Gunilla is going too. She can stand to listen to fart stories because she's a feminist. She can come too, but only as far as the base camp at the house."

"What about Mischa?"

"Sure. Mischa is coming. We need a strong team. Fast, brave dogs and smart, tough kids."

"Is that what we are?"

"That's right. And we're all going on this expedition together."

Mina could feel how her heart was pounding.

"Great, Grandpa," she said. "Awesome."

But there was one thing that Grandpa didn't tell her. For a long time he had wanted to climb Three Cave Mountain, which stood east of the house in Värmland. But it wasn't something that you could do alone.

And Mischa, that black-and-white East Siberian *laika*, Grandpa's dog, knew something that no one else knew since they had been up there in July. There was a secret up there in the forest, or maybe a danger threatening, up on Three Cave Mountain.

Mischa sensed something. Or maybe she wanted to warn them.

CHAPTER 3

Setting Up
Base Camp No. 1

1.

*T*HE HOUSE IN VÄRMLAND WAS BIG AND OLD AND STOOD near a lake. There were meadows leading down to the lake, and that's where you could plant potatoes.

It's fun to plant potatoes, thought Mina. In the fall she was allowed to go along and dig up the potatoes, which made her back ache. But then they would take a break and eat raspberry pie. Gunilla was the best at digging up potatoes because she had such short legs and it was easier for her to reach down. One time a snake appeared on the path down to the potatoes. Gunilla screamed, and ever since then Mina and Moa had to wear boots because Grandpa said the snakes had short teeth and couldn't bite through the boots.

The house in Värmland was very close to what was called Norway, and in the past there were Germans there. In the old days Germans were nasty, and that's why the

Swedish army had built a fort on the land near the house in Värmland. The nice Swedish soldiers were supposed to stay in the fort and defend the country. When you were defending, it meant that you weren't scared, and you fired guns at the attacking forces, and if you were good at scaring them, the Germans would leave you alone. But that was back then. Nowadays all the Germans were nice, said Grandpa, because he had written a book that all the Germans had bought and he got lots of money so he could buy a Benefactor dog. And now the Germans were practically feminists who cleaned up without being asked, said Grandpa. But back then, in the past, they were mean and fired guns, and that's why people had to build a fort and defend themselves if the Germans came.

The fort stood across from the potato field. It was nothing more than a hollow in the ground with a railing in front, and the soldiers could lean on it when they were defending themselves. A tank trap stretched from the fort all the way down to the lake. The trap was made from piles of big rocks, so that when the Germans came, their tanks got stuck. Then they had to sit there in their tanks that were stuck and feel like idiots and ask for help, but they didn't get any help, no siree.

But things weren't like that anymore. That was in the past, and now birches and Scotch pines had grown over the fort. The Germans weren't nasty anymore. Instead they

read books and were feminists and helped with the cleaning without being asked.

That was how Grandpa and Gunilla had explained everything.

It was there, to the house in Värmland, that Grandpa and Gunilla and Mina and Moa and Ia and Marcus had driven, with Mischa and the new puppy in the back. Värmland was practically a wilderness. There were forts and wolves and bears, and that was where Grandpa and Gunilla drove with the children, headed for what would be the horrible adventure of climbing Three Cave Mountain.

2.

Nobody knew what Grandpa had said to the children's parents. In any case, he didn't say anything about a horribly dangerous expedition "that would unite the team and make men of them all," or however he thought about it. But two days after the terrible night when the crocodile bit Mina on the butt, Grandpa and Gunilla were sitting in the car, driving to Värmland. It was a big car, and on the back seat sat Mina, Moa, Marcus, and Ia.

In Västerås they had picked up the puppy. Mina was allowed to choose one of the five puppies. It was hard to choose. But then one of them came over to her and gave her a pleading look, and she knew that was the one. The puppy had a face like a scrub-brush, and she stuck out her tongue and licked Mina.

The puppy was now named Elsa, after Grandpa's aunt whose name was Elsa and who had lived to be ninety-two. Grandpa had always liked her. The first thing they did after arriving in Värmland was to baptize the puppy. To baptize someone, you had to pour water over them and say a magic spell like this: "In the name of the Father and the Son and the Holy Ghost I baptize you Elsa Gilbertsson. May success and happiness follow you on all the seven seas." And then you had to drink a toast with raspberry juice and dry off the puppy with a towel.

Elsa had a mustache and bangs and fantastically beautiful almond-brown eyes. When they were driving to Värmland, she lay close to Mischa, who was so happy. Mischa thought she had been given a little baby, and she licked Elsa up and down, so she was practically soaked, but at least she was clean. Once in a while Elsa would stand up and pee in the car, and then all the children would clap, but Gunilla got mad and said that it was starting to stink like hell. But then Grandpa said: Just wait until she starts pooping. Then Gunilla would really have something to smell.

And Elsa sat down and pooped in the car, but it just smelled like mustard, said all the children, who were on Elsa's side.

At a place called Våtsjön they stopped to take a break. Grandpa stuffed little Elsa under his jacket and took her along inside the restaurant, where dogs and smoking were not allowed. There he ordered meatballs with mashed potatoes for everybody, and when the waitress brought the plates, she looked surprised and said, "Are there seven of you? I only see six."

Then Grandpa said that Gunilla, his wife, was pregnant and could give birth at any moment. Neither Gunilla nor the waitress thought that was very funny. But as soon as the waitress was gone, Grandpa hauled Elsa out of his jacket and set her on the table. And Elsa started gobbling up the food.

All four kids followed her lead. They licked their plates clean, because the children didn't want to set a bad example.

When Elsa was done, she burped, so all the kids burped too. Marcus was the loudest.

Marcus was five years old. He had blue eyes and blond hair and he sounded a little hoarse when he talked. Grandpa said that he had a poetic nature, even though he was probably going to be a hockey player. But he was the youngest, except for Moa. And the girls, meaning Ia and Mina, thought he was rather cute, and that's why they tyrannized him, or so Gunilla always said whenever she had to separate them. She said Marcus was always getting pounded because he was so beloved.

He was the only boy among the "cuzzes." They said "cuzzes" instead of "cousins." Marcus was taller than Moa but shorter than the other two. He was a lot shorter than Ia, who was his big sister, and that was hard to take. His sister Ia had started giving him instructions, telling him what he did right and wrong, mostly wrong. Sometimes he would go nuts and punch her in the stomach and then his sis would give him a pounding.

The first night in the house in Värmland they slept on mattresses on the floor because all the kids wanted to sleep together, and nobody wanted to sleep in a bed because then they couldn't sleep with the dogs. That was the first night that Elsa was away from her mother. Whenever Elsa would lie down, she would feel sad and start to cry. She had such pretty brown eyes that filled with tears that spilled out and completely soaked her mustache. Then Mina held little Elsa in her arms and pulled the blanket over the puppy and petted and stroked her until she calmed down and stopped crying. And Marcus lay on the other side of her and stuck his nose in Elsa's fur. So all four kids lay there with two dogs, and that's how they slept on the first night.

When Mina woke up and Grandpa asked her what she had dreamed, Mina said she hadn't dreamed about anything. And no crocodile had bitten her on the butt. But she still had an uneasy feeling in her stomach.

She didn't tell anyone about this, except for Mischa. She whispered in Mischa's ear something that only a faithful, East Siberian *laika* could keep secret. She knew that she could trust Mischa.

"I'm a little scared about this expedition," she told the dog.

3.

The next day Grandpa was going to take the four children and the two dogs on the first stage, the first part of his plan for climbing Three Cave Mountain.

That was the name of the mountain that stood east of the house near the town of Helgeboda. It was more than thirty-three hundred feet high. But they weren't going to climb that high on the first day, only up to the first cave, the one behind three small birch trees that grew nearby and made it easy to find the entrance.

Grandpa had a knapsack because the idea was to set up a base camp in the first cave. None of the kids knew what a "base camp" was, but Grandpa explained it to them before they set off. If someone was going to do mountain climbing that was very difficult, like for instance climbing Three Cave Mountain, which was over thirty-three hundred feet high, then it couldn't be done all at once. It was too far and too hard. They would get too hungry. And Elsa's paws would start to hurt if she didn't have a chance to rest. So they had to take breaks, for example at the first cave. And there they would find food. There they could rest and eat.

That's why they had to take food and other necessities up to the first cave, which would be the base camp.

Then they would go back home, and on the following day they would go farther up the mountain, after resting and eating at the first cave's base camp. That's what people did on mountain climbs that were really difficult.

"Great," said Marcus. "I saw on TV what they do when they climb the Himlamaya."

"Himalaya," said Ia. "Not Himlamaya."

"Well, anyway, they climbed up something called the Himlamaya," said Marcus in a grumpy voice.

"You're too little," said Ia. "You don't understand anything. Nobody does when they're only five years old."

"But I saw it on TV when I was two," said Marcus. "And at that age you know a lot!"

Then Ia and Marcus starting fighting, as usual.

But Grandpa said: "If you're heading out on a great

big expedition, you can't be fighting. Everybody has to stick together! Enough!"

"Himla-maya," said Marcus. "Himla-maya, Himla-maya, Himla-maya!"

By ten o'clock everyone had calmed down. Grandpa packed his knapsack full of necessities, and they all set off for the first cave.

Grandpa had the knapsack on his back, and he was wearing the baby carrier in front. The baby carrier was for the puppy Elsa, who was too little to make it all the way on her own. She might have been able to do it, but she kept on leaping back and forth, and there was no controlling her.

That's why she was now riding in the baby carrier on Grandpa's stomach. He had borrowed the carrier from Gunilla's youngest grandchild, whose name was Skrutten. He was only eight months old and had stayed behind in Stockholm. Elsa kicked around a bit but then got used to it, and she was now riding in the carrier, peering out at everything and humming, and she seemed very happy.

"Pay attention now," said Grandpa, "because there are wolves and lynxes and bears around here. Keep your eyes open."

"What does a bear look like?" asked Marcus. "Is he big?"

"You'll know when you see one," said Ia. "Keep quiet now. You're scaring the little birds."

"But what does he look like?"

"He's as big as an elephant except a lot smaller. Now be quiet, Marcus!"

Marcus walked behind everyone else and thought things over for a long time. Then he said:

"I see a bear over there."

Everybody stopped. They were walking along a path that sloped gradually upward, and they had now climbed for some distance so that they could see the valley below. Everyone looked. Moa went over to Grandpa and hugged his knees.

She looked scared.

"Where?" said Ia.

"Over there," said Marcus. "There's a bear."

Everybody looked. It was, absolutely positively, a big rock.

"You dummy!" said Ia. "That's a rock. Can't you see that? And it's gray, while bears are brown, and besides they move, but a rock doesn't!"

Marcus looked at the rock for a long time.

"I see a bear," he said. "There."

"Marcus!!! That's a rock. Now that's enough!" said Ia.

"But I see a bear anyway," said Marcus.

"You have a poetic nature, Marcus," said Grandpa. "Now let's keep going."

And they started off again, up toward the first cave. First Grandpa with Elsa in the baby carrier. Then Mina and Moa in a row. Then Ia, who was holding Moa's hand. And last Marcus.

It was such a magnificent day. And no one had the slightest idea about all the horrible things that were going to happen.

Suddenly they saw the cave.

It was dug into the mountainside, right at the foot of the slope. It was almost hidden behind three small birch trees, but they could see entrance.

Grandpa went inside. The cave was thirteen feet deep, six-and-a-half feet high, and running along one side was a stone ledge that you could sit on. A little stream trickled out of one of the cave walls, which, as

Grandpa explained, could be a big help if you had to stay in the cave for a long time in an emergency. Then you would have water.

"What's an emergency?" asked Moa.

"It's when you feel threatened," said Grandpa, "and you have to hide out in the cave. So let's unpack and bunker down and set up the base camp."

Then Grandpa began setting up the provisions for the base camp.

He had brought along plastic bags and little boxes, and he lined up the necessities at the very back of the cave. First the drinks: four bottles of Coca-Cola, two bottles of Pepsi, two orange Fantas, and two blueberry Fantas. To these he added a pint of chocolate milk and two pints of yogurt. Then came six little chocolate cakes with nuts, two bags of Daim candy bars, a package of lollipops (fifteen green and fifteen red), and two packs of long sausages and a jar of mustard. Also two packages of raspberries and one of strawberries with a half pint of cream, a bag of sugar, six paper plates, ten plastic spoons, ten cups, ten knives and forks, a bowl and a package of dry food for Mischa, and a bowl and two cans of dog food for Elsa, who wasn't used to dry food. Plastic bags (for picking up poop from the cave floor in case little Elsa had an accident), and a package of Marie biscuits, twelve chocolate cookies, a bag of zwieback, and a pound of butter. Finally, one bag of mixed candies (a pound and a half) and four comic books.

"Here are the provisions for our base camp," said Grandpa. "Is there anything missing? Think carefully."

All the children thought for a long time.

"Ice cream," said Marcus, "with chocolate syrup."

"Oh, what a dummy you are," said Ia. "Don't you know that ice cream would melt in the heat? You can't have ice cream at a base camp. Try to use your head a little, Marcus."

"Well, anyway, ice cream," said Marcus.

"MARCUS!!!" said Ia.

Grandpa just said:

"Marcus is right. We should have ice cream. But Ia is right too. We can't have ice cream at the base camp. But the third cave is cold. It's up above the tree line. There we can have ice cream."

"With chocolate syrup," said Marcus.

"Exactly," said Grandpa.

"There, you see, Ia," said Marcus. "I was right again."

They went out and sat down at the mouth of the cave.

They all sat in a row: Grandpa, Mina holding Elsa on her lap because that's what Elsa liked best, then Moa, Ia, and Marcus. And at the very end of the row was Mischa, holding paws with Marcus. They all thought it was a rather solemn moment. They sat there in total silence, looking out over the valley. Far in the distance they could see Grandpa and Gunilla's house, with smoke curling up from the chimney.

At last Marcus said:

"I've been wondering about something—and here it is. I wonder if you could bicycle up that big pine tree."

Ia promptly replied in a very kind voice, as if she were talking to an idiot:

"Marcus, you can't bicycle up a pine tree. That's impossible."

"But what if . . ." said Marcus, "what if you imagined that you could bicycle up a pine tree. Then . . ."

"But you can't bicycle up a pine tree."

Marcus was starting to get mad, and for a moment he didn't say a word, and no one else said anything either. They all just looked out over the valley at the forest and the smoke coming from the house far away. But finally Marcus said:

"Yes, but what if you imagined that you could bicycle up a pine tree, all the way up to the top, and so . . ."

"MARCUS!!!" said Ia. "Now you're being stupid. You're five years old and you should know that it's impossible to bicycle up a pine tree. That's enough!"

"Yes, but," said Marcus, almost on the verge of tears, "what if you COULD bicycle up a pine tree, then . . ."

"MARCUS! ENOUGH!!!"

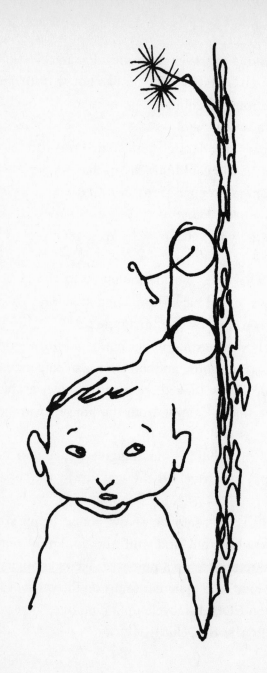

But just as Ia and Marcus were about to fly at each other and start fighting, Grandpa said:

"Marcus, you shouldn't start crying, and you shouldn't fight. You have to argue your case!"

"What does that mean?" asked Marcus.

"Argue your case. You have to explain what you're thinking, and why you're thinking that way. Why you're saying that it would be fun if you could bicycle up a pine tree. You have to EXPLAIN to Ia what you mean. Don't just start wailing. And above all don't start punching."

"Is that what it means to argue your case?" said Marcus.

"Exactly. You have to argue your case. Then Ia will understand what you're thinking. Explain to her what you mean by bicycling up a pine tree."

"But it's impossible . . ." began Ia. Then Grandpa told her to keep quiet because Marcus was going to argue his case.

"Should I start arguing now?" asked Marcus.

"Right," said Grandpa. "Go ahead."

Everyone looked at Marcus. Now he was going to argue his case. They saw that Marcus was biting his lip and thinking hard.

"Come on, go ahead!" said Ia. "You're supposed to argue your case now and explain what you mean by bicycling up a pine tree."

"Yes, let's hear it," said Grandpa kindly.

Everyone waited with anticipation to hear what Marcus would say. They could see that he was thinking hard. He was biting his lip. Then he said:

"I see a bear."

Everybody went completely nuts.

"MARCUS!" shrieked Ia. "You're supposed to ARGUE YOUR CASE!!! Don't start in on that now. You're driving me crazy!"

But Marcus was just staring straight ahead, and he said again:

"I see a bear."

"Marcus. Sweet, sweet Marcus."

But then Marcus raised his arm and pointed, and said simply:

"There."

And everybody turned, almost against their will, to look in the direction that Marcus was pointing. And then they saw it.

A bear.

It really was a bear, and he was just like Grandpa had said. He was as big as an elephant, although much smaller, but he was big enough, and brown, and he lumbered slowly past them only ten yards away. The bear was so close that you could have thrown a pine cone at him, but nobody dared. Everyone sat in total silence, like statues, and also a little scared. The bear was ten times the size of Mischa, and suddenly he stopped and looked

at them as they sat there, Grandpa and four kids and two dogs all in a row outside the first cave, the one that was only a short way up the slope and was now their base camp with tons of provisions.

The bear stopped and looked at them as they sat there all in a row. No one said a word.

And then, at that very instant, Mischa raised her head straight up in the air and started to howl. It was a long song, aaauuuuuuuuuUUUUUUUuuuuuuuu, and it rose and fell, because that's exactly the way all sled dogs howl who come from the Siberian tundra far, far away to the east.

The bear stood motionless, looking at Mischa.

Then the bear raised his head too, stood up on his hind legs, and then they saw that the bear was taller than Grandpa, even though he was over six feet tall. And the bear answered. It was like a bellowing, dark and rumbling. It sounded like rrrrrrrrRRRRRRRRRrrrrrmmmmm. And Mischa fell silent.

Not another sound was heard.

Then the bear got back down on all fours. And started walking away. Slowly he walked up the mountain.

Everybody was still sitting perfectly still.

"What did he say?" Marcus said at last.

But Grandpa was still sitting in silence and didn't reply. They could see that he was worried, and the children knew that Grandpa could probably understand what the animal had said. Finally he told them:

"He was nervous. A problem has come up," he said. "He was nervous."

Then he stood up, picked up Elsa, and stuffed her into the baby carrier. He took Moa by the hand and said:

"And I am too. There are hunters in the valley. It's strictly forbidden to shoot lynxes and wolves and bears, but some people are evil. There are people in Germany who hunt endangered animals and sell them, and there are people like that in Håvilsrud, Sweden too. Maybe even in Arvika. I don't know. The bear wanted to warn us. But he was nervous. Now we have to go home to Gunilla, because a troubling situation has come up. There might be some danger, and we need to discuss things."

CHAPTER 4

The Wolf Cub
in Trouble

1.

OF ALL THE CUZZES, IA WAS THE ONE MINA LIKED BEST. IA was actually given the name Cecilia back when she was baptized and they said the magic spell: "May success and happiness follow you on all the seven seas." Ia was three years older than Mina, and she liked taking care of her younger cousin. Ia was fun to play with, and she had nice eyes. It was only when Ia fought with her brother Marcus that things got difficult.

That evening, as they made the long trek home from the mountain and their encounter with the bear, both Ia and Mina could tell that something was up with Mischa.

The dog kept sniffing at the air and barking.

Mischa may have been old, but she had an amazing sense of smell. Grandpa said she could smell a fart from seven hundred yards away, and tell who it came from. Marcus once went down to the road and let loose a little fart. Then he stood there, waiting for Mischa to appear and say it was him. But after a while he got impatient and went back to the house, where he found Mischa lying on the floor asleep.

And she was grumpy when Marcus woke her.

"How dumb do you think I am," was probably what she said. "Try and understand. I want to sleep. Try and understand."

Marcus thought he recognized that part about "try and understand," but he couldn't remember who was always saying that. Finally he did remember. It was Pappa, when he wanted to sleep in the morning. Then he would keep on saying "try and understand" and refuse to get up. Marcus had talked to Mina about this, and she told him that's the way grown-ups were. They would say "try and understand" and then turn over and start snoring. You just had to get used to it, Mina said. But she thought it was too bad that a great dog like Mischa would say such a thing.

They made the long trek down to the house from base camp number one in the first cave, and Grandpa looked worried but didn't say anything. Some kind of danger was in the works. Mischa was worried too. She stopped several times to sniff the air.

They finally reached home, exhausted. Gunilla had started to worry. She always worried whenever Grandpa went off on dangerous expeditions, and this time he had taken all the children along. She stood in the doorway, grumbling, when they arrived, but she was relieved.

"And I bet you're all really hungry. How am I going to fix you all something to eat at this hour?" she said but then rushed off to the kitchen.

"Women are tough," said Mina, because that was something that she had learned to say from Gunilla in difficult situations.

Then Gunilla, who was quite a fun person, gave Mina a hug.

But things were strange. By now it was dark, and the forest around the house on the side facing the mountain was completely black. And Mischa was uneasy. She stood on the porch, staring into the darkness and sniffing the air.

"What is it, Mischa?" asked Marcus. "Why are you so worried? Is there something out there?"

But Mischa didn't answer. She just stood there with her nose in the air, sniffing at the menacing darkness.

Something was up.

2.

The next morning Mischa had disappeared.

No one knew how it had happened, but a window on the first floor was open. She must have jumped out. Little Elsa, the Schnauzer puppy, had slept in the double bed with Mina and Moa. All night long she had burrowed her

snout against Mina's ear so it tickled, and Mina hadn't gotten enough sleep and said "try and understand" when Moa wanted to play. But then she heard the others talking, and Grandpa was shouting that Mischa had disappeared.

Suddenly she was wide awake.

"Mischa ran away," said Marcus, who was sitting on the porch and staring at the forest and the mountain.

He had tears in his eyes. He'd been sitting on the porch all morning, calling, but no Mischa had appeared.

"There was something going on yesterday," said Grandpa, who had come outside. "But Mischa will come back. Something must have been calling her."

"A thing can't call," said Ia. "Who do you mean by 'something'?"

"We don't know. We'll just have to wait and see."

And so they started waiting. This was the day when they were supposed to go up to base camp number one before they made the final attempt to climb the mountain. But they couldn't set off before Mischa had come back.

"We all have to stick together," said Grandpa. "We have to wait for Mischa."

And so they waited.

＼

That was the day when Pip and his mother, Lotta, were due to come to the house.

Lotta was Gunilla's daughter. She had a week's vacation and was going to leave Pip in Gunilla's care. Gunilla was Pip's grandmother, and she was a little nuts about how great Pip was. Pip was only eight months old and couldn't even walk yet, but Gunilla said he was beautiful, wonderful, talented, and completely extraordinary, practically a miracle. Whenever she talked about Pip all the other kids would start yawning. Once Marcus had even pretended to fall asleep, but then Gunilla got mad, even though she was really a fun person who liked jokes. Mina actually thought that Pip was okay, though not quite as wonderful as Gunilla always said. But one time Mina said that whenever she looked at Pip it made her think of Grandma Vega's potato dumplings, which were so fantastic. Pip looked just like a happy little dumpling.

Gunilla didn't think that was very funny.

Anyway, in the middle of the day Lotta and Pip arrived. And then Marcus asked whether Pip was going to come with them to climb Three Cave Mountain. And Mina, who remembered her dream about the cannibals in the Congo, suggested that they take Pip up to base camp number one and gobble him up if their provisions ran out, because he looked so plump and good, especially with ketchup.

But Lotta, who was Pip's mother and had a short fuse, as people say—whatever that means—got really mad.

Why were they joking like that when it wasn't very funny? And just then, they were talking about Pip, Marcus started to cry.

"I love Mischa so much. What if she doesn't come back," he said and kept on crying. He was inconsolable.

"What if the hunters shoot her?"

And when he said the word "hunters" everyone suddenly fell silent. And no one wanted to joke anymore.

At 2:30 in the afternoon, Mischa came back.

She was completely soaked, and she had a cut on one ear, but otherwise she was perfectly fine. And it was clear that she had something to tell them. She was in such a nervous state and so worn out that it was almost impossible to understand what she wanted, but she absolutely refused to go inside.

She tugged at Grandpa's leg, dashed out to the porch, stopped, ran back, and wanted to set off again.

"We have to see what she wants," said Grandpa. "I need two kids to help me. Is there anyone who wants to volunteer?"

"Aubbbbbbb psss bubbbb," said Pip, who had crawled out onto the porch.

"Sorry," said Grandpa, "you're too little."

"I'll go with you," said Moa.

"Sorry, that won't work either," said Grandpa. Then he looked at Mina and Marcus and Ia, who were all standing with their hands raised.

"Mina and Marcus will come with me," he said. "Ia is in charge of home base and has to be ready to help out."

"You're not supposed to say 'help out'," said Mina in a bossy tone of voice. "That's what Gunilla says. It's supposed to be self-evident."

"Okay, okay," said Grandpa, a little annoyed. "But that only applies to cleaning up. We have to leave now."

Mina looked at the forest. Before it had seemed so nice, with the birches growing over the fort, and the beautiful pine trees, and beyond them the slopes rising up, one higher than the other. And beyond everything you could almost see the fabulous mountain that had such a strange but beautiful name: Three Cave Mountain.

But now the forest they were about to enter was almost—menacing.

For a moment Mina thought about the way things used to be, meaning back home, before they came up here to the house in Värmland, which was called Söderås. Back then, if she was scared, she would start howling and Pappa or Mamma would come. But now things were actually much worse, although she wasn't howling. It didn't seem the right thing to do in the situation. They all had to stick together and go into the forest, which seemed almost menacing, to find out what Mischa wanted. Until they found out, they wouldn't be able to complete the expedition to Three Cave Mountain.

"Are you ready, girls?" said Grandpa. "Fasten your bras and let's get going!"

That's what they always said in the Norrland Rifleman Corps when Grandpa was in the military.

"Very funny," said Ia.

"Let's go," said Mina.

And then they set off through the forest, which was on the way up to Three Cave Mountain, heading for whatever it was that Mischa wanted to show them.

3.

Mischa took off as if she weren't one hundred and nineteen years old. Sometimes she would stop, impatient, and wait for Grandpa, Mina, and Marcus. And when they caught up to her, she would set off again without a sound.

Something was urgent.

It was hard to walk because it had rained in the night and the ground was soggy. And if they touched any branches, a shower of water would completely drench them. After an hour they suddenly heard Mischa baying.

"Baying," said Grandpa. "Mischa has found something."

"What does 'baying' mean?" asked Marcus. But then his eyes lit up and he pointed and said:

"Look over there! I see a baying!"

"Marcus," said Grandpa, "baying means when Mischa, who is an elkhound, finds an elk, for example. Then she barks so that we'll know. You can't *see* baying. You hear it."

"But anyway, I see a baying," said Marcus and pointed.

And there, a hundred yards away, stood Mischa. She had found the spot. And she had something to show them.

Cautiously they moved forward.

Mischa pointed her muzzle at something that was lying inside a rock crevice a few yards away. It was a wolf. The wolf lay motionless, and when they got closer they could see that it was dead. There was blood on him and they saw that the wolf had been shot. The bullet had entered his chest, but the wolf had not died instantly. They could see traces of blood on the ground. The wolf had tried to drag himself away to hide, but didn't make it. And then he died inside the rock crevice.

But he must have managed to go a good distance, because the hunters who shot him hadn't found him.

"Was it the hunters that the bear told us about?" asked Mina, and then she began to cry.

"Damned murderers," said Grandpa. But no one told him he shouldn't swear, because they all felt the same way, even though they weren't swearing.

"I think so too," said Marcus, and his lower lip began to quiver.

It was a big wolf, almost a giant, they thought, and beautiful as he lay there with closed eyes. It was awful to see, because he must have suffered terribly. But Mischa seemed impatient. It wasn't the dead wolf that she wanted to show them. She jumped up on the rock. Behind it grew a little fir tree with branches reaching all the way down to the ground.

There. Something was there.

Marcus was the first one to understand. He crawled up the same way, lifted up the branches, and saw what it was.

"Grandpa!" he cried. "Come and look!"

Grandpa and Mina went up onto the rock and bent down under the branches.

There they saw a little muzzle peeking out and a pair of eyes peering at them. A tiny little creature that was shaking all over.

It was a little wolf cub.

She was as small as a cat. She had been following

along with her pappa, who had now been shot. The hunters hadn't seen the wolf cub, who didn't dare leave her pappa's side. She didn't understand that he was dead. And then she found a hiding spot near her dead pappa. The night must have been awful, cold and wet, because the wolf cub was soaked through and shaking horribly. She was completely exhausted and could hardly move.

Grandpa bent down and picked up the wolf cub. He turned the cub this way and that, examining her carefully. The little wolf cub was so exhausted that she didn't kick or struggle. She didn't offer any resistance at all as Grandpa examined her.

"She's not injured," said Grandpa at last. "The hunters probably didn't know that there was a wolf cub too. They were just after the big wolf, and they missed the cub."

For a moment he stared at the big dead wolf, and then he shook his head.

"How strange," he said. "It's the pappa they shot. The mamma must be all right. She must be around here somewhere, but in hiding."

"Where?" asked Marcus. "We have to find her."

"I don't know," said Grandpa. "But she's probably lying in a wolf den, waiting for the hunters to go away. She probably doesn't know that this little one is still alive. She must have had her other cubs to look after."

"Maybe she doesn't have any other kids," said Marcus.

They thought a moment about what Marcus had said. And then they thought about what the wolf mamma must be thinking right now. And it was awful. The wolf cub pressed close to Grandpa. Mina took off the green scarf that her mother had given her as a birthday present and began drying off the cub.

"We got here just in time," said Grandpa. "The cub wouldn't have made it through another night."

"I'm thinking of calling him Rubert," said Marcus.

"It's a girl," said Grandpa.

"Then I'm thinking of calling her Maja-Rubert," said Marcus.

And since Ia wasn't there to tell him that a girl wolf couldn't be named Maja-Rubert, no one objected.

"What are we going to do?" asked Mina.

"We have to go home," said Grandpa. "Maja-Rubert has to get warm and dry. And above all, she has to go back to her mamma."

The wolf cub looked at them with eyes that were frightened and worried, and her little body was still shaking all over. But Mina kept on rubbing her with the scarf. Soon the wolf cub was almost dry.

"We'll call the police," said Grandpa. "It's a crime to shoot wolves. We'll have to leave the wolf pappa here. He's dead, but there will be a criminal investigation. The hunters have to be punished. But we'll take the cub with us."

Suddenly Mina thought of something.

"Mischa! We forgot to thank Mischa!"

And then she jumped down to Mischa, who was sitting motionless at the base of the rock, and she gave Mischa a giant hug. They could see how happy this made Mischa. She was also a little embarrassed because she was rather shy, but she was happy too. And everyone knew that if Mischa hadn't made them come out to the forest, the little wolf cub might not have survived another night.

And then they headed back to the house.

4.

Gunilla was standing on the porch holding Pip in her arms, and she saw them coming. Grandpa was carrying the wolf cub inside his overalls. Then he opened his overalls and pulled her out.

Gunilla almost dropped Pip on the ground.

"What's that?!" she said. "Where did you find her?"

Grandpa told her all about it. Gunilla's face turned

solemn, because she understood what might have happened. While they were away she had started to worry.

But what were they going to do with the little wolf?

The cub didn't utter a sound, and just kept looking at everything.

"I think her mamma is somewhere up there in the forest," said Grandpa. "Or up on the mountain. We have to take her back. It will be better for her up there. But she needs time to recover. She's practically done in."

Ia had already thought of that. She had started heating up some milk. She dragged a quilt out of a cupboard, and she found a bag of dry cereal in the pantry. Ia was very determined. It was as if she had suspected what Grandpa was going to bring back home, even though she couldn't have known. And she was very good at planning. She and Gunilla began looking through books to find out what wolf cubs liked to eat, but they couldn't find anything.

"What rotten cookbooks," said Gunilla.

Marcus and Mina were already busy making a bed for the wolf cub. It was important for her to get warm. Marcus made a fire in the fireplace, and Pip crawled in big circles around the wolf cub, uttering little noises that the other kids thought was wolf-talk, because the cub started looking at Pip, at first a bit scared but then in surprise.

"Shall we put Pip and the little wolf baby in the same bed?" asked Marcus.

"Why?" said Moa.

"Because babies like to sleep together!" said Marcus.

Then Ia brought a bottle that she had borrowed from Pip, and Mina picked up little Maja-Rubert and held the cub in her arms. Ia held the bottle, Marcus scratched the cub on the tummy, and Moa held out a towel in case Maja-Rubert threw up. The fire blazed in the fireplace, and the cub's eyes grew heavier and heavier, and just as she finished half the bottle, her eyes fell shut and she began sucking slower and slower. All the kids were watching intently.

At last the wolf cub fell asleep.

The fire crackled. Maja-Rubert slept. And then Mina carried the little wolf cub to bed, carefully pulling the blanket up to the cub's neck, and all four children stood around the bed. No, all five if you counted Pip, but he hadn't gone along to rescue the cub, and he didn't understand what a horrible experience it had been. Even though things had worked out fine. Soon Pip fell asleep in his crib.

But that evening the other four children sat for a long time around the wolf cub, who slept soundly and securely. And they all thought that Maja-Rubert was the most wonderful and beautiful wolf cub they had ever seen.

But what was going to happen to her? What was going to happen?

That night a strange sound woke Mina.

The room was dark. The fire in the fireplace had gone out but the embers were still glowing faintly. The other kids were asleep in their beds, but Mina had lain down in the wolf cub's bed so that Maja-Rubert wouldn't be scared if she woke up and started to cry for her mamma, the way Mina used to do. Then a sound woke up Mina.

It was a long, plaintive song: oooouuuuuuuuuuuuu-uuuuuuuuuuuuuuuuuuuaaa. And then it faded away and started up again: oooouuuuuuuuuuuuuuuuuuuuuuuuuuuu-uuuuaaa. Silence. Then the plaintive song came back, faintly, from far away.

Suddenly Mina understood. It was the wolf cub's mamma calling for her. She was calling and calling for her child. Mina turned her head and looked at the wolf cub. Maja-Rubert was awake too. She was lying there with her eyes open, staring up at the ceiling. She had heard it too.

Her mamma was looking for her, and calling.

The cub had her paws on top of the blanket. Mina put out her hand and took one of the cub's paws, holding it quietly. The call rose and fell, faintly, very faintly. Finally it stopped.

Mina looked at the wolf cub. She had heard it. She knew that her mamma was calling for her baby, and searching. Finally Mina saw the cub's eyes starting to droop. Eventually she closed her eyes, and Mina heard from her breathing that she was asleep. But Mina kept holding the cub's paw so that she would feel safe. And then, at last, they were both asleep.

In the morning the cub was up earlier than anyone else.

She had ambled over to Pip's crib and stood there looking through the slats. She seemed to be wondering what kind of creature was inside.

Pip had stuffed his thumb in the cub's mouth, and he was happy and laughing. The children spent all day brushing the cub's fur and stuffing food into her. Mostly porridge, but she also liked Coca-Cola when they poured some in a dish. Grandpa sat at the table, brooding and saying very little, but Mina told him what had happened during the night. That made him even more thoughtful.

"She's searching for the cub," he said. "Next time we hear the mamma calling, we need to be on the alert."

"Can't Maja-Rubert stay with us?" asked Ia. "I like her so much."

"That won't work," said Grandpa. "A wolf needs to live in the forest and in the mountains. And just think

about her mamma. She's going around up there on the mountain, searching and feeling desperate."

"So what should we do?" asked Marcus.

Grandpa looked at Mischa in silence for a moment. Then he said:

"Mischa was once almost a wolf," he said. "Her great-great-great-grandmother was a wolf on the Siberian tundra. I think Mischa knows what she has to do."

For a long time he looked at Mischa, who was lying on the floor at his feet. And then he said:

"You know, don't you, Mischa? You know what you have to do."

Mischa didn't make a sound. She had played with the cub for a while, but grew tired. Now the cub was batting around a ball of yarn.

"Mischa," said Grandpa, "do you know what you have to do?"

And after a while Mischa got up and left the room. She went out the front door and across the lawn and jumped up onto the big flat rock that stood at the edge of the forest. And then Mischa raised her head in the air and started to sing. It was a long, one-note song; a long, deep, beautiful one-note howl, that sounded like: oooouuuuuuuuuuuuuuuuuuuuuuuuuuuuuuuuaaa. And then she lowered her head to listen. She raised her head again and sang.

No one had ever heard her sing that way before. It sounded a little sad, almost eerie, but really very beautiful. And Mischa sat there on that rock for almost half an hour. All the children stood on the porch and listened, and nobody said anything, because they understood that something very strange and remarkable and maybe even magnificent was about to happen.

And then, after a long silence, they heard it.

Far away, almost as if it came from the very top of Three Cave Mountain, someone was answering. A faint song, a howl, that rose and fell.

"It's her," said Grandpa. "It's the mamma. Now she knows."

"What does she know?" asked Mina.

"She knows where her little cub is. And I think she's on her way here. She wants to take Maja-Rubert home."

"Will she get to do that?" asked Mina.

"Mischa has promised her," said Grandpa. "That's what she was singing. And a promise has to be kept."

"What do we do now?" asked Marcus.

"We wait."

And then the long wait began.

5.

The afternoon passed, then the night, and another morning.

The wolf cub was practically the most splendid and beautiful thing they had ever seen, but she was a little uneasy. She had trouble sleeping that night and woke up often to listen with her ears pricked.

But on the second night there wasn't a sound. Not a sound from a mamma wolf who sang and called. What had happened?

Was it the hunters?

Then, at dusk on the second day, she came.

They were all sitting in the kitchen around the big table. Gunilla and Grandpa and the five children.

Mischa was lying under the table the way she always did, because by mistake someone just might drop a little piece of sausage. It was strange, but Marcus always seemed to be dropping slices of sausage by mistake. No one really knew why. Mischa was not allowed to beg, so that she wouldn't get in the habit of being fed at the table; she only got food in her bowl. But strangely enough, Marcus often dropped little tidbits. Then Gunilla would give him a sharp look and say that it was odd how clumsy he was getting. And he wasn't at all the clumsy sort.

Marcus said that he couldn't understand it either. Then Mischa would burp under the table. And Marcus would get such a strange look on his face, almost cross-eyed.

The wolf cub was sitting on Mina's lap, gobbling up some liver sausage from Mina's finger. Elsa was sitting with Ia. And then, just when they were all chatting with each other and feeling so comfortable, they heard it.

It was powerful, and very close. There could be no doubt. Oooooooouuuuuuuuuuuiiiiiiiiiiiooooooommmmm. It was a song, as if from a wolf, as if from a wolf mamma who was calling to her cub.

And she was very, very close.

They went out on the porch, and they saw her at once. She was a big wolf, and she was standing at the edge of the forest, up by the little mound that had once been a fort but was now overgrown with pine trees and birches.

She was the mamma wolf. She was standing perfectly still, looking at them. Grandpa was holding the wolf cub in his arms.

"What should we do?" asked Marcus.

"Let her go," said Mina. "We have to let her go back to her mamma.

Then Grandpa cautiously set the wolf cub down on the ground. For a moment she peered up at them, at Grandpa and the children and Mischa and Elsa, as if she were wondering what they wanted her to do. Then the wolf mamma sang again: ooooouuuuuooooo. But only briefly. And the wolf cub heard it.

She took off running across the lawn as fast as her little legs would carry her. And then she reached the wolf mamma.

For a brief moment the wolf mamma looked at her, as if she weren't quite sure that the cub was really alive, or as if she were so happy that she almost didn't know what to do. But then she began sniffing. First she sniffed and then she started licking Maja-Rubert from her head all the way down her back.

"She's washing off our smell," said Marcus.

Then the wolf mamma turned around and walked into the forest, and the cub followed close behind, very close. But before they disappeared, the mamma turned around and paused for a moment to look back at them.

It was as if she wanted to thank them. And then the mamma and her cub were gone.

"Where are they going?" asked Ia.

"Home," said Grandpa.

"Where's their home?" asked Ia.

"I don't know," said Grandpa.

That's when Marcus started to cry—not hard, but his lower lip began to quiver and tears welled up in his eyes. But then he pulled himself together, sniffled a little, and said:

"I can see where they live."

"No, you can't, Marcus," said Ia. "That's impossible."

"Yes, I can," said Marcus. "Sometimes you can see right through a forest and through a mountain, and that's what I can do, and I see where they live. But I'm not going to tell."

And no one dared contradict Marcus because he had been right so many times that they didn't really know what he might be able to see. He had stopped crying now. Dusk had come and soon it would be dark, and the wolf mamma and her cub were gone.

"I think we'll see them again," said Grandpa. "I don't know when. But tomorrow we're going to resume our expedition up Three Cave Mountain."

And then they went inside the house. And they all had a feeling that the next day was going to be very, very exciting. But Mischa was awfully quiet, as if she were brooding about something that no one else could know.

CHAPTER 5

The Expedition Resumes

1.

By the time Mina came downstairs from the children's bedroom on the following day, Grandpa had already been up for a long time. And he had packed.

He had rolled two double sleeping bags together and fastened them to the top of his knapsack. Fastened to the bottom were the ground cloths. And Gunilla was standing nearby, looking worried.

"I'm not happy about you going," she said. "And it's so nerve-wracking that the cell phone doesn't work up there on the mountain. What if something happens? Then you won't be able to call anybody. And you're going to be gone for three days!"

"I don't think anything's going to happen," said Grandpa.

"You don't think! But what if something does happen?!"

They ate breakfast and hardly anyone said a word at the table. When they were finished, they were supposed to have a conference out on the steps. "A conference" meant that Grandpa would tell them about everything that was going to happen and what they were going to do, and then the kids could ask questions, and they would all decide on things together.

Mischa lay on the floor with her head pressed flat and her ears sticking straight up. It was obvious that she was extremely tense.

"Today," said Grandpa, "we're going to begin an expedition that I think will take three days. We could do it in two, but I don't think that would really be enough time. We're going to conquer Three Cave Mountain, and we're going to do it together."

"What does 'conquer' mean?" asked Marcus.

"Climb to the top," said Ia.

"Who's going to go along?" asked Marcus, looking uneasy.

Grandpa glanced around and took a deep breath. Then he said:

"Well, first of all Mina, since it's really because of her that we're going on this expedition in the first place. And Moa. I hope she'll be able to keep up, but of course we'll take breaks and rest, so I'm sure she'll be fine. And

Marcus and Ia. I've given a lot of thought to the dogs, but I think we'll only take Mischa along. Elsa is too little. It would be best for her to stay home and protect Pip and Gunilla."

Everyone nodded solemnly. No, Elsa's little paws probably wouldn't be able to make the climb up the mountain.

"Everybody needs to wear boots," said Grandpa. "And nobody should be hungry when we leave. And no one should be scared."

They all looked at him in surprise.

"Why should we be scared?" said Ia.

But Grandpa didn't answer. And all of a sudden Mina felt something inside that told her this might not be so easy. Maybe there was even good reason to be a little scared, just a little.

Why else would Mischa be standing on the porch and gazing up at the mountain so nervously? In some ways dogs understood a lot more than humans did. Dogs had instincts. And they could see through forests and mountains. Maybe they could even see into the future.

Maybe Mischa sensed something. But she wasn't telling them. And Mina felt a lurch in her stomach, not so much that it made her scared. But it felt as if she were standing up on a high rooftop and looking down, and she could sense how very high up she was. That's how the lurch in her stomach felt.

And then they set off. Gunilla, Pip, and Elsa stood in the doorway and waved. The final expedition to Three Cave Mountain had begun.

2.

They reached the base camp at the first cave around five o'clock that afternoon, and everything had gone well. They had taken a break almost every half hour because the kids had never learned to go to the bathroom all at the same time. They had to keep taking bathroom breaks, and finally Grandpa said:

"If only you would all take a lesson from Mischa. She just stops and takes a pee once in a while." He sounded a little grumpy.

"But Mischa doesn't wear any clothes," said Marcus.

The base camp looked exactly the way they had left it five days earlier. They were anxious to see if their provisions were still there, and Marcus ran the last hundred yards to get there first. He dove into the cave and came out with a Daim candy bar in his mouth.

"The provisions are still here!" he said and stuffed the whole candy bar in his mouth so they could hardly understand what he was saying.

The cave was only a hundred yards up the side of the mountain, practically at its foot. Grandpa was breathing hard the last part of the way; his knapsack was quite heavy. But at last they were all inside.

The floor of the cave was nice and clean, with just a few old leaves and branches. Lined up along the stone shelf on the far wall were all their supplies.

Nobody had touched them.

"Roll call!" said Grandpa. He took off the knapsack and sat down on the floor. All the children and Mischa sat down in a row in front of Grandpa.

"First, crew check!" he said. "We'll start on the right and each of you will say how you're feeling and whether you have any injuries. Okay, go ahead!"

Moa was the one farthest to the right.

"Moa wants ice cream!" she said.

"Good," said Grandpa. "That means Moa is her normal self. What about Marcus?"

"Well, I was thinking that when we went fishing yesterday, I thought my perch was smaller than Ia's, but now I think maybe I was wrong, because mine was probably a pike, and a pike is always bigger than—"

"Marcus!" said Ia. "You're supposed to tell us how you're feeling!"

"If I get to the top of this mountain, I think I'm going to fly home because if I hold out my arms, like this—"

"Marcus! You can't fly like that!"

"But what if I could? Then I'd do it. But my legs wouldn't be so tired if I ran into an angel who could act like a motorbike and then—"

Ia and Marcus were just about to start fighting again. Grandpa raised his arms and said:

"Okay, this is what we're going to do. If anyone has blisters on their feet, raise your hand!"

No one raised his hand.

"Is anybody tired?"

Everyone raised their hand except Mischa, who was lying on the floor and seemed to be asleep.

"Is anybody hungry?"

"YESSSSSS!" they all bellowed so that Mischa woke up and bolted to her feet.

"Good," said Grandpa. "Now we're going to prepare to spend the night here."

He started unpacking his knapsack, and Mina, who wasn't as tired as the others, helped him. They spread out the ground cloths, and on top they placed the two double sleeping bags that were each big enough for two grown-ups. They were actually six, if you counted Mischa, but Moa was so little that there should be plenty of room.

But before they crawled inside, they were going to eat.

It turned out to be a fabulous feast. Grandpa divided everything into five identical portions, and the first thing they did was start trading. For example, a hot dog with ketchup could be traded for a Daim candy bar. Or someone who didn't like Coca-Cola could trade it for a Fanta, or trade raspberries for strawberries, and lollipops for chocolate cookies. And that's what they did for half an hour until everyone was finally satisfied. Except for Mischa, who sat there with her dry food, looking glumly at her bowl until Grandpa waved his hand with a magic flourish and pulled out of his pocket a handful of meatballs. Suddenly Mischa was in a much better mood, and everyone started eating.

"Now remember," said Grandpa, "that you're never supposed to give Mischa anything at the table if she begs. But I ask you, is this a table?"

"NO!" they all shouted in unison.

"Exactly," said Grandpa. And he stuffed his hand into his other pocket and pulled out more meatballs for Mischa.

"But there's still no need to tell Gunilla about this," said Grandpa. "Because she'll just say that I'm spoiling Mischa. Are you going to tell on me?"

"NO!" they all said in unison.

"Good," said Grandpa. "Then we'll all pledge solidarity."

"What's that?" asked Marcus.

"That's when you don't tell Gunilla about something," said Grandpa.

And then they all went back to eating.

By seven o'clock dark had fallen, and they crawled inside the sleeping bags.

Grandpa and Marcus were in one of them; in the other were Ia, Mina, and Moa. At first Mischa wanted to sleep outside the sleeping bags, but after a while Moa started feeling sad and began to cry. Then Mischa crawled inside next to her, and Moa burrowed her head into Mischa's fur and stopped crying.

It quickly grew very dark inside the cave. And Grandpa said:

"Tomorrow is going to be a hard day. We need to be rested to conquer the mountain. Now we'll say our evening prayer and sing."

And then all six of them said:

God who loves children
one and all,
watch over me,
since I'm so small.

Wherever in
the world I land,
my fortune lies
within God's hand.

Happiness comes and happiness goes.
The one God loves, his happiness grows.

And then Grandpa sang a song he knew, which went like this:

Heaven and earth may burn
Heights and mountains vanish,

But whoever believes will find
That the promises are forever.

When he was done, it was pitch dark inside the cave.

Marcus was snoring very, very faintly. And after a tiny little moment, Mischa chimed in and started snoring in her own way: puuueeeeee, puuuueeeee, pueeeeeee.

Mina was the last one to fall asleep. She missed her mother.

3.

When Mina woke up, Mischa was standing at the mouth of the cave, looking out at the valley. It was raining lightly, drizzling, and the clouds were hovering so low that only the tops of the closest trees were visible.

Grandpa slowly hauled himself out of the sleeping bag.

"What crummy weather," said Marcus from deep inside the sleeping bag. "Are we really going to conquer the mountain today?"

"Absolutely," said Ia.

"Absolutely," said Moa.

There didn't seem to be anything wrong with their spirits. They all ate breakfast in silence. Grandpa pulled out rain gear for everybody from his knapsack. Gunilla had guessed that it might rain and supplied the rain gear, and they were all grateful for that.

At ten o'clock they set off.

The climb got steeper now. The path to the top of the mountain was very narrow, and they walked slowly. First Mischa with Mina, then the others, with Grandpa following behind. The pine trees got shorter and shorter. Grandpa said that they would soon reach the tree line: there it was so high up that no trees could grow. It was very cold up there, and only moss and tiny flowers grew. After a while the rain stopped, but the fog still hovered low overhead.

But it wasn't fog. They were now so high up that they were actually walking inside a cloud.

They may have been walking inside a cloud, but it felt like walking through white milk. It felt both eerie and solemn. They all knew that they were very high up now, but they couldn't see anything down the mountainside.

"When we come up above the cloud," said Marcus, "will we be able to see angels?"

"We'll have to wait and see," said Grandpa. "We'll know soon."

"Can I borrow an angel?"

"Why would you want to do that?" asked Grandpa, huffing and puffing.

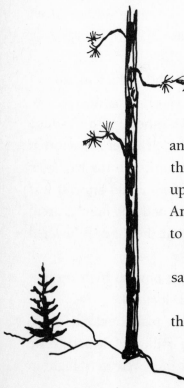

"Well, then I could use the angel as a motorbike, and then she would flap her way down with me on her back, and then it wouldn't be such hard work."

"Stop babbling about angels, Marcus! There's no such thing as an angel," said Ia. "Not up here, anyway. You're just lazy. And besides, no angel would want to fly with you."

"I think I can see an angel," said Marcus. "Almost, anyway."

"Oh, come on!!!" said Ia. But then Grandpa told them to stop fighting because it was hard enough work as it was.

And then, all of a sudden, they were through the cloud.

They came out of the cloud and saw Three Cave Mountain quite clearly, and the top was very close. Beneath them lay the cloud like a white sea. Yes, they had really gone through the cloud and come out above it. But the sun was not shining. There were more clouds overhead, but they had come through the lowest cloud.

The top of the mountain was three hundred yards ahead. And they could see, very clearly, two caves just below the peak. They looked like two eyes staring down at them. It was kind of eerie.

"Is that where we're going?" asked Mina.

"Exactly," said Grandpa. "And when we get there, you'll understand why you'll never in your life have to be afraid of a green crocodile again."

"Really?" said Mina. "How will I know that?"

"Because," said Grandpa.

And then he started on the last part of the trek. Until now Grandpa had always gone last, to make sure that none of the kids was left behind. But this time he went first, and he seemed to be especially eager because he practically leaped for the last precipice. His knapsack was big and heavy; it was so big that Grandpa was almost invisible from behind. And then he set off, climbing up the last part of the path toward the two caves. The cloud they had come through still hovered below their feet, and the clouds overhead were still there too. But in between they could see the top of Three Cave Mountain quite

clearly. And everything was utterly silent. It was no longer raining. Grandpa climbed upward, moving very quickly, as if he were impatient. Beneath their feet the cloud hovered like a big milky sea, and ahead of them was the top of the mountain with the two caves like two black eyes, staring down at them.

At that instant, when Grandpa was only a few yards from the mouth of the cave on the right, something terrible happened.

Maybe it was because it had rained and the rocks were slippery. Or maybe it was because Grandpa was so eager to reach the cave. But suddenly one of his feet slipped and he staggered. For a moment the kids saw him reeling, wildly flailing his arms in the air to regain his balance. And then he fell.

He fell down the rocky slope, dragging loose stones with him and making an awful crashing noise in the silence. Then he landed with a loud thud in the crevice of a rock.

They could hear him moaning faintly, and for a moment the kids thought he had been killed. But then they saw him twisting and turning. His face was all contorted, as if something hurt terribly, and then they heard him saying something.

"You clumsy oaf," he said to himself. "Now you've done it, you clumsy oaf."

And they realized that disaster had struck.

* * *

Marcus was the first to dare approach him.

Grandpa was lying motionless on the ground. He was still wearing the knapsack on his back, and he looked up at Marcus with an odd little smile, as if he hurt terribly but was also joking a bit, almost as if he wanted to apologize.

"How are you?" asked Marcus.

Grandpa grunted a little and tried to free himself from the knapsack. But something was hurting him terribly and he stopped.

"I think I've broken my leg," he said. "Yes, I think that's the problem. I've actually broken my leg."

"Does that mean we're walking back home?" said Marcus.

Grandpa tried to laugh but it sounded odd, not at all like his usual calm and good-natured laugh.

"I don't think I can do that," he said. "I wish I could."

"So what are we going to do?" said Mina. And you could tell by looking at her that she realized what had happened was really terrible, that something very, very terrible had occurred, because her voice quavered when she spoke.

And then, at that very instant, it started to rain. This was not a light drizzle but a heavy downpour, a truly miserable rain, and suddenly they saw that it wasn't just rain but sleet, rain mixed with snow, and it felt cold and miserable.

Suddenly they were all scared.

It was as if Grandpa no longer had an answer to

every question. He was lying there on the ground with his face contorted, and he was trying to take off the knapsack.

"Grandpa," said Moa and started to cry.

What were they going to do? Grandpa finally managed to get the heavy knapsack off. He lay on the ground, panting loudly and looking up at the cave that he had missed by only a few yards. The snow mixed with rain was falling harder. They felt cold and miserable. They had been walking for five hours from their base camp at the first cave, and now Grandpa had broken his leg.

And what were they going to do?

"We have to go up there," said Grandpa. "We have to help each other. Otherwise we'll freeze to death if we don't seek shelter in the cave."

"But you can't walk," said Marcus, crying in despair. "How are we . . . how can we . . ."

Grandpa stopped groaning and looked at him.

"Marcus," he said, "what if you could bicycle up a pine tree? Can you picture that?"

Marcus just kept sobbing.

"Just picture it!" said Grandpa. "Just imagine if you could bicycle up a pine tree."

"Yes, but . . ."

"Well, then we can get up there too. I can't bicycle or walk, but I can crawl. Okay?"

"Okay," said Marcus and stopped sobbing.

"Good," said Grandpa. "If you take the knapsack, Mina and Ia will help me crawl."

And then they started off.

4.

Afterwards they could hardly remember how they managed to get Grandpa up there.

It must have taken almost an hour to go those twenty-five yards back up to the cave. Ia and Mina dragged Grandpa. He slid along on one side and you could tell by looking at him that the broken leg really hurt. He dragged it behind him, muttering the whole time about what an idiot he was and why had he brought the kids out here, and now he had only himself to blame. It was very wet.

Behind them followed Marcus, hauling the knapsack up the steep mountain path, inch by inch.

"Keep trying, Marcus!" Grandpa said now and then.

As if they weren't all trying. Because of course they were.

At last they reached the cave.

It was bigger than the first cave, which was now base camp number one, but the entrance itself was smaller, about three feet across. Inside it was pitch dark, but Grandpa slid through the mouth of the cave with a louder groan than they had heard for the past hour. Ia and Mina tumbled after him, followed by Moa and Marcus and the knapsack.

Mischa came in last. Mischa's fur was completely soaked. They had now reached the second cave on Three Cave Mountain. They were inside.

Only then did they start to look around.

It was so dark that they could hardly see a thing. And they didn't really expect to see anything. They knew that the cave was empty. They were quite sure about that.

But there was something strange about it; they could suddenly sense it.

Grandpa merely lay on his back, huffing and puffing. But Marcus thought he caught a glimpse of something, and Mina thought she could hear something that sounded like a faint peeping or whimpering and then a low hissing. But that could just be Mischa, who was now sitting outside, looking anxiously at the mouth of the third cave, which was fifty yards away.

Yes, there was something strange.

Suddenly Marcus pointed toward the back of the cave, but he didn't say a word, just pointed. And everyone looked.

Then they saw in the dark a pair of eyes gleaming at them. A pair of eyes that shone bright yellow and did not move, fixing them with an angry glare from the darkness of the cave. All the children saw it. And finally Grandpa also turned his head and saw what they saw.

In a flash they all knew what it was because gradually their eyes were growing accustomed to the dark, and just as gradually they saw the contours of a wolf, a big wolf, next to the far back wall of the cave. A wolf was staring at them with intensely glowing yellow eyes.

A wolf. They had entered a wolf's cave. And Marcus kept on pointing, as if he had discovered something else. And then they saw something else. Because right below the glowing yellow wolf eyes, which belonged to a very big wolf, they saw a second pair of eyes. Not as big. No, much smaller, like those of a smaller wolf, maybe quite a little wolf.

And then they instantly understood.

It was a wolf cub.

CHAPTER 6

The Wolf Murderers Attack

1.

LATER ON, THAT WOULD BE THE MOMENT MINA REMEMbered best of all: the way they sat there in utter silence on the floor of the cave in the dim light and then saw that not only was there a big wolf mamma in the cave, a big wolf that might be dangerous and ready to attack them, but also a little wolf, a wolf cub.

And it was a wolf cub they knew.

They realized this when the wolf cub suddenly gave a start and began moving, toddling across the floor toward them. The cub went over to Mina and started sniffing at her. First her hand. Then her pants. The cub climbed up on her, sniffed at her face, and then, as if only now did she recognize someone she knew as a friend, she cautiously licked Mina's cheek.

"It's Maja-Rubert," whispered Marcus.

That's when Mina started crying again. Not because

she was sad. But because she had been terribly scared, and now she was so happy.

Grandpa lay on the floor, not making a sound. It was obvious that he really would have liked to groan, but he held back because he didn't want to scare the kids.

The wolf cub was very lively and happy, scampering around and greeting all of them. But after a while the wolf mamma stood up. Slowly she came over to the cub, lifted her up by the scruff of her neck, and carried her back. The kids watched, now feeling a little calmer.

Both the wolf mamma and her cub seemed to remember what had happened: that the kids and Mischa had rescued the cub. But even so, the mamma was a little suspicious. When Mischa cautiously padded over to them to say hello to Maja-Rubert, the wolf mamma opened her mouth and said something that sounded like: AAAAaaaaauuuup. It was almost like a burp, and then Mischa cautiously backed away, pretending that she wasn't scared at all, and was just yawning. She also shook her coat and pretended that it was raining, which it was outside the cave.

"Open the knapsack," said Grandpa. "Take out the ground cloths and the sleeping bags and spread them out on the floor. We have to get warm."

Ia and Mina got started at once. Everybody was freezing, everybody was hungry, and the more they thought about things, the more miserable they felt. Grandpa was injured and couldn't walk. The cell phone didn't work up here on the mountain. It was raining, and in a few hours it would be dark.

The situation was a disaster.

The children took off their rain gear and shoes and crawled inside the sleeping bags. They instantly felt better. Even Marcus, who was a shiver-expert and often felt cold because he was so small and skinny, stopped shivering.

Grandpa cautiously sat up and felt his leg. His face was very pale. The slightest touch on his broken leg hurt. They could see that because then he opened and closed his mouth, the way Pip did when he wanted to nurse.

Yet not a sound crossed Grandpa's lips, not even a little smack. And he looked awful.

"Now listen here, kids," said Grandpa at last. "This is how things stand. We're in a bad situation, but nothing is hopeless. We'll make it through the night all right. But we have to get a message to civilization."

"What's civilization?" asked Marcus.

"Gunilla," said Grandpa. "At this moment, my dear children, Gunilla Thorgren, fifty-eight years old, is civilization. For the only time in her life. But we're not going to get a message to her tonight. And no one expects us home before nighttime on the day after tomorrow. Tonight we'll try to survive here, along with the wolves. But early tomorrow morning . . . then we'll have to . . ."

And he fell silent.

"Do you have a plan?" asked Ia.

"Yes," said Grandpa. "The leader of an expedition always has to have a plan in case disaster strikes. I do have a plan. But first we need to get through the night without freezing to death."

"What are we going to eat?" asked Marcus, who was almost always hungry.

Grandpa sighed heavily.

"We have two Daim candy bars and eight chocolate cookies. Plus hot dogs and a pound-and-a-half of candy. That's all. We're not going to get fat on it. But we're not going to die, either."

"As long as you have a plan, Grandpa," said Mina. "Do you have one?"

"Yes, I have a plan," said Grandpa.

That's when Marcus said: "I'm thinking of giving my chocolate cookies to Maja-Rubert."

Everyone looked at him. Everyone suddenly thought that he was an incredibly nice boy, but they were still a little surprised.

"Then you can have half of mine," said Ia.

And then Marcus gave her a slightly embarrassed smile, and it was as if they had never fought in their whole lives, as if Ia had never said "MARCUS!" in a shrill and angry voice. It was as if everything had now changed, and they had become brother and sister, and they would always, always stay together and never fight again.

And so they got ready for the miserable dark night that they would remember forever.

2.

Dark fell early, and the rain kept coming down.

The cave was pitch black. Mina couldn't sleep, and she realized that Grandpa couldn't sleep either. Occasionally he would moan, although very softly. They had placed the two sleeping bags on either side of him to keep him warm. He had tried to crawl inside the biggest bag, but he couldn't do it because of his broken leg. But if they put the sleeping bags on either side of him, he would be warmer, and after a while Mischa decided that she would lie on top of his stomach.

Then he was plenty warm.

Mina lay for a long time looking into the darkness of the cave. She saw the big wolf's two yellow eyes glittering at her, but after a while the wolf mamma's eyes started to blink, and the two yellow eyes disappeared. Then Mina realized that the wolf mamma was asleep. She could hear the other kids breathing calmly, as if they were sleeping, and after a while she felt something touch her cheek, something soft and warm.

It was the muzzle of the wolf cub.

Cautiously, very cautiously, Mina opened the top part of the sleeping bag, not wanting to wake the other kids. The wolf cub was breathing lightly against her cheek. Then she felt the cub crawl up to the opening of the sleeping bag and climb in next to her.

"What do you think your mamma will say about you sleeping here?" whispered Mina.

No answer. The wolf cub just nudged her shoulder with her muzzle, nestled into Mina's armpit, sighed, and fell asleep.

Mina cautiously zipped up the sleeping bag again. Now it was warm. Grandpa was awake, but he wasn't freezing, and he had Mischa on top of him like a blanket.

Then Mina fell asleep. She didn't dream about anything, not about crocodiles or about cannibals. She just slept deeply and quietly with the wolf cub in her armpit.

3.

Mina woke up because someone was moving about.

It was Grandpa. He had lifted Mischa off of his chest, sat up, and was regarding his broken leg with a gloomy expression.

It was now daylight outside. The rain had stopped, and the mouth of the cave was like a bright round opening. The night was over. Mina tried to remember whether they had actually eaten anything. Then she saw a bunch of empty wrappers from the chocolate cookies spread all around, and an uneaten cookie over by the place where the wolf mamma had been sleeping.

But the wolf mamma wasn't there. She had gone out. Maybe she doesn't like chocolate cookies, thought Mina. But she didn't say anything, just lifted the wolf cub out of the sleeping bag.

"Your mamma is going to come back soon," said Mina in the grown-up voice she had learned from her mother. "She's gone off to work but she'll be back soon. Don't worry. Do you usually go to nursery school?"

The wolf cub just looked at her, and it was clear she thought that was a strange question because she didn't answer.

"We all have to get up," Mina heard Grandpa say. "It's time."

"Do you have a plan?" asked Marcus in a voice that sounded very little and weak and scared, coming from the other sleeping bag.

"Yes," said Grandpa.

"A plan that will rescue us?"

"Yes," said Grandpa.

"Good," said Marcus in his new scared voice. "Good. Awesome."

And then Grandpa explained the plan that was going to rescue them from their emergency situation.

*   *   *

It might have been about eight in the morning. Normally, on an ordinary day, Moa and Marcus would be on their way to nursery school, Ia and Mina would be headed for school, and Mischa would be out taking a stroll with Grandpa.

But this was not an ordinary day.

"I can't move," said Grandpa. "My cell phone isn't working. And we have to get in contact with civilization."

"You mean Gunilla," said Marcus rather proudly, because he remembered what Grandpa had told him.

"Yes, Gunilla. And then she'll contact the people who can help us get down from here. Especially me. I think it's going to have to be a police helicopter. But somebody has to go back down to the house. And it's a five-hour hike, and not an easy path. Moa and Marcus couldn't do it, and I'm afraid that . . ."

Grandpa fell silent. Then he said:

"Ia, do you think you could walk back down? You can't go alone; you have to take Mischa with you. Mischa can find the way, and you're the biggest and strongest of the kids. You have to sound the alarm. Do you think you can do it?"

Everybody looked at Ia. She was sitting on the floor, scratching the wolf cub behind the ears. And then she raised her head and looked at the others. Everyone was staring at her. What was she going to say? It was a long walk down to the house. It was a difficult hike that

would take five hours down to base camp number one, and it was almost the same distance down to the house.

"Can I take Mischa with me?" she asked.

"You have to take Mischa," said Grandpa. "Otherwise I won't let you go."

Then Ia nodded and said simply:

"Okay, I'll do it."

Five minutes later Ia was ready to go.

No one said a word, but they stuffed her pockets with two Daim candy bars and a chocolate cookie, along with five meatballs for Mischa, in case she got tired, and they handed Ia her rain gear.

"Should I keep Mischa on a leash?" asked Ia.

"Yes," said Grandpa. "Mischa is going to lead you home. Mischa is the one leading you, and not the other way around. You have to stick together. No matter what happens."

Everyone went over to Mischa and scratched her behind the ears to say goodbye. Mischa looked solemn but very calm. Ia didn't say much, but Mina saw that her lower lip was quivering slightly.

"We're counting on you," said Mina.

Marcus stood at the mouth of the cave and looked at his sister. Then he went over to Ia and gave her a big hug, and he said:

"Women are tough."

Because that was something he had heard you should say when faced with something that was inhumanly difficult. And he had tears in his eyes.

Then Mischa and Ia set off on their long and difficult rescue mission to get help for those who were stranded on Three Cave Mountain.

They all stood outside the cave and watched as Mischa led Ia down the mountain. Two small dots that grew smaller and smaller and finally disappeared completely.

4.

The sun came out in the middle of the day, but still no wolf mamma.

Maja-Rubert was getting more and more uneasy and had started whimpering. Marcus took the last chocolate cookie and mixed it with some water that trickled out of the cave wall. He tried to give the wolf cub some of this chocolate soup with a spoon from Grandpa's first-aid kit. The cub ate a few spoonfuls but then refused any more.

Mina began singing "Itsy-Bitsy Spider," but that didn't cheer up anyone.

"Maybe we should prepare ourselves for another night here," said Grandpa.

Then Moa started to cry.

That was when, at about five in the afternoon, they heard the gunshot.

It came from far away, and yet maybe not.

The sound ricocheted between the mountains, and it took several seconds for the echo to fade away. They all rushed to the mouth of the cave, except for Grandpa, of course, and gazed out across the valley. Clouds had moved in again over the forest and valley. The forest below the mountain was completely covered. It looked like a white quilt right below them. The mountain was like a huge ship sailing on a white sea.

And then the sound of the gunshot vanished.

"What was that?" asked Mina.

They sat and waited, holding their breath. It was very quiet. The only thing they heard was the sound of the wolf cub whimpering more and more anxiously, until finally she raised her head in the air and started howling. They had never heard the wolf cub howl before, but now she did: uuuuuuuuUUUUuuuuuuuu. Quietly and sadly, and then the cub fell silent.

That's when they saw the wolf mamma. She came racing up the mountainside from the right. She seemed to emerge from the white sea, leaping from rock to rock, moving so fast up the mountain, up to the cave.

"It's the hunters!" screamed Marcus. "They're trying to shoot her!"

Now the wolf mamma had reached the cave. The wolf cub started spinning like crazy, around and around, and the wolf mamma took Maja-Rubert by the scruff of her neck and lifted her into the cave, practically tossing her inside. Then she came out again, took up a position at the cave's entrance, and gazed out across the valley.

Nothing moved down there. But that's when they saw that she was bleeding.

It wasn't a big wound. But they realized at once that a bullet had very nearly given her a serious injury. It was like a thin bloody streak along one side of her neck. The shot had grazed her fur yet hadn't gone deep. But the wound had started to bleed.

"She's bleeding," said Mina. "Do you have any Band-Aids, Grandpa?"

"Band-Aid," said Moa and held out her index finger the way she always did. "Moa wants a Band-Aid!"

"Get the knapsack," said Grandpa from inside the cave.

In his knapsack Grandpa had a first-aid kit—a box

of medicines to be used in an emergency. Mina crawled inside and together they dug out a bottle of disinfectant. That's what they always used when anyone got a scrape. It stung like crazy and in the past, before everything with the crocodile and the expedition and the accident with Grandpa happened, Mina used to scream like a pig whenever it was dabbed on. But that was a long time ago, that was before all of this happened. From now on Mina was never going to scream like crazy about almost anything again.

Mina came out holding the little bottle of disinfectant and a cotton ball. She went over to the wolf mamma, opened the bottle, poured the disinfectant onto the cotton ball and said to the big wolf that was standing there, keeping an alert eye on the valley below:

"It's going to sting at first, but you're so brave, I know you can handle it."

The wolf mamma turned her head and looked at Mina as if she couldn't believe her ears.

"All right," said Mina, "it's going to burn now."

And afterwards Mina would many times recount how amazing it was: that the wolf mamma didn't give a single sign to show how it stung, not a sound, although maybe she did flinch a little, just a little. But not a sound. Hardly even a blink of her eye.

"Oh, how brave you are," said Mina. "Now the wound is clean. Now it won't get infected."

And then, right at that instant, they saw the hunters approaching.

5.

All the children dashed inside the cave. Last came the wolf mamma. She headed straight for her spot at the very back of the cave, placed the wolf cub against the cave wall, and stood in front to protect her.

"They're coming to shoot her," said Marcus.

"Take it easy," said Grandpa. "They don't know that we're here."

"So what?" said Marcus. "They're murderers."

"Maybe they'll get scared when they see you," said Mina, trying to make a joke.

Marcus just looked at her. And then, as if it were suddenly totally unbearable to see the wolf mamma and her cub pressing themselves against the back of the cave, waiting for the hunters to come and shoot them, Marcus suddenly seemed to have an idea.

He jumped up, dashed out of the cave, and took up a position on the little ledge that jutted out in front of it. The two hunters were very close now, only fifty yards away, and they were climbing faster and faster toward the cave, as if they knew that the wolf was inside.

Marcus stood up and then he started waving both arms and he screamed as loud as he could:

"YOU DAMN MURDERERS!!!"

His words echoed through the mountains.

The two hunters stopped as if paralyzed and stared up at Marcus. What was this?! What kind of madman was this?

"We see who you are!" he started yelling again. "YOU DAMN WOLF MURDERERS!"

The two men exchanged a few words, then one of them shook his head. Both had rifles. It was clear that they didn't know what to do. They had been hunting a wolf and were almost certain that they had wounded her. And that they had her cornered inside the cave.

But now a little boy wearing boots and green rain gear was standing up there hollering.

"THE POLICE will be here soon. We've SOUNDED THE ALARM!" he screamed. And now the men were talking to each other again, and one of them shook his head and started climbing upward.

"Keep quiet," said Grandpa from inside the cave, but Marcus had no intention of keeping quiet. He was on the verge of tears, but then he started in again, bellowing:

"The police helicopter is on its way . . ."

He didn't really know what else to say, but then he started up again, shouting:

"And then you're going to be TORTURED!"

Now the second hunter had started to climb upward. It was pointless. Everybody inside the cave was going to be killed. Along with the wolf mamma. And Maja-

Rubert. But then, suddenly, a strange sound was heard.

The men stopped. They looked up at the sky. And there, far in the distance, they saw a black dot that was getting bigger, and Marcus saw it too. It was like a buzzing black bird flying just above the cloud cover, above the white sea, and heading for Three Cave Mountain.

It was flying fast. Not with wings, but with the buzzing blades of a helicopter. And it was getting closer, and they saw what it was: a police helicopter.

"POLICE" it said in huge letters on the side of the helicopter. And then the hunters turned around and started desperately running down the mountain. One of them fell, dropped his gun, and stared up at the helicopter as it made a steep turn.

The other hunter kept running and was finally swallowed up by the sea of fog. But the first one was having trouble moving. He sat down and rolled around, as if in great pain.

The police helicopter was flying above him in ever tighter circles.

CHAPTER 7

The Third Cave

1.

IA DIDN'T REMEMBER THE ROUTE THEY HAD TAKEN UP the mountain, but Mischa did. Now they were headed down the same path, and it was steep. If they didn't make it down before dark, they would be lost.

On the hike up, Ia had mostly walked along looking at her feet and at the rocks, but Mischa had spent the whole time looking around, and now she remembered everything. It was easy to see that her ancestors had been sled dogs in Siberia. She lowered her head, pulled steadily at the leash without yanking on it, and never looked back.

Mischa, thought Ia, everything depends on you. You have to find the way. The others are sitting up there in the cave and they're counting on us. Mischa, you have to find the way.

But she didn't say a word. She simply followed Mischa, who steadily pulled at the leash.

No, Mischa wouldn't let them down.

* * *

It was no longer raining, but Ia felt as if she were walking through thick milk.

She thought to herself that now she knew what it felt like to be a dog on a leash, because Mischa was the one who decided which way they would go. They had walked down through the white cloud and couldn't see more than a couple of yards ahead. It was awful. Not a sound to be heard except for water trickling down the mountainside and stones clattering. And Mischa, who was panting ahead of her and who seemed to know exactly which way they should go.

Then they came out of the clouds, on the underside, and could see better. Ia took a short break every hour; otherwise she wouldn't be able to keep going, and that's what she told Mischa. Then Mischa would sit down at her feet and look up her uneasily.

"Don't worry, Mischa," Ia told her. "I'll make it, but I just have to rest once in a while."

Once she started to cry because she was so tired, but Mischa stood up on her hind legs and licked her face, and then Ia had to laugh in spite of it all. After that she was fine.

The worst thing was that Ia got blisters on her feet. Once she sat down and took off her boots and then she saw that her heel was bleeding, but she shook the boot up and down and emptied out the blood, without crying. She just said "CRAP!" because that was something she had heard her pappa say when everything was really miserable.

Then they started off again.

Her legs felt completely numb. Several times she fell down and scraped her hands. Each time Mischa would stop, and it was clear that she was worried. One time when Ia fell and almost didn't have the strength to get back up, Mischa started shaking all over. Maybe she

was tired too. Maybe she was afraid that Ia wouldn't keep going.

Then Mischa licked Ia's face. It was as if she wanted to say: "Don't give up. Women are tough."

But of course she didn't say that. It was just Ia who sobbed and then staggered to her feet and said:

"I'm okay, Mischa. Let's go."

And so they continued on, slower now, but they both knew that they had to make it down the mountain before dark fell.

It took them eight hours to reach the house.

Ia was soaked with sweat and the palms of her hands were both bloody. From a distance Mischa had already started barking to get Gunilla's attention. She came out on the porch with Pip in her arms and almost screamed when she realized what had happened.

Mischa went inside and drank water from her bowl. Ia just sat down on the porch, huffing and puffing and staring straight ahead and not thinking about anything except that she had made it. Gunilla called the rescue service in Karlstad. And the police.

"How are we going to find them?" said Gunilla. "They don't know where the caves are."

"Don't worry," said Ia, "I do. They're in the second cave. I'll go along in the helicopter. There are three caves on the mountain. The first one is base camp number one with our provisions. That's not where they are. The second cave is the wolves' cave. That's where they are."

"So what's in the third cave?" asked Gunilla.

"I don't know," said Ia. "We didn't go inside that one."

"Why not?" asked Gunilla.

"I don't know," said Ia.

And then they heard the sound of the rescue helicopter coming from Karlstad. It swung in from the west, over Lake Vällen, which was below the house, across the town of Helgeboda, and down toward the house called Söderås. And it landed on the lawn to pick up Ia and Mischa, the two who would show the way to the group stranded in the second cave on Three Cave Mountain.

2.

The helicopter lifted off and rose up through the cloud: off in the distance Three Cave Mountain loomed, and the mouths of the two caves were visible high up on the mountain, like two black eyes looking out across the valley.

Ia gazed into the distance. She stood next to the two pilots and pointed, and in front of the cave on the right she thought she could make out a little boy with blond hair gazing up at them.

That had to be Marcus. The strange thing was that

she could also see two strangers. One of them was running down the mountainside, in wild flight, and soon disappeared into the cloud that covered half the mountain. And there was another person who fell, dropped his gun, and was still lying there.

"It's the hunters. It's the wolf murderers!" she screamed into the police officer's ear.

He looked down, the helicopter swerved, he nodded.

"We've been after them for a long time," he said.

Then he put in a call to the other helicopter.

They had plenty of time to catch the wolf murderers now—they wouldn't get away. But first they had to rescue the group stranded inside the cave. The helicopter flew in a wide circle around the top of the mountain, looking for a landing spot. And they were in luck. Right above the wolves' cave there was an open space, on the very top of the mountain. The helicopter slowly sank toward the space, its motors roaring. As the helicopter neared the ground, grass and twigs flew in all directions, and with a thud it landed on the mountain top.

They had arrived. Ia went over to the edge and looked down, and there stood Marcus, waving wildly and happily, and then the others came out, one by one, and the kids were reunited.

The pilots from the rescue helicopter went down to the cave with a stretcher, carrying it inside to Grandpa.

He was lying on the floor, looking grateful. He was even more grateful when one of the pilots took out a syringe with some pain-killing medicine and stuck it in his leg. He said: OOOoooooufff and smiled for the first time in three days. Then they carefully lifted him onto the stretcher and carried him up to the helicopter.

Mischa stayed with him the whole time, as if to supervise that everything was done properly.

"You did it, the two of you," said Grandpa to Ia.

"I couldn't have done it without Mischa," she said, sounding tremendously grown up. "I mean, we did it together."

"I wouldn't have lasted another twenty-four hours," said Grandpa.

"Sure you would," said Mina, who was listening. "You could have done it. A person can do a lot more than he thinks."

And then Grandpa didn't say another word, because he knew that was true, but he hadn't known that Mina knew it too. So that's why he didn't say anything.

And then the pilots put him inside the helicopter.

It was time to say goodbye to the wolves. The kids took each other's hands and went inside the cave, which had once seemed so terrifying, and yet it had saved their lives. They went inside the cave together to say goodbye to the wolf mamma and the wolf cub.

One by one they gave the wolf cub a hug. The wolf mamma watched. To her they merely nodded, because they had respect for her, and Marcus simply said, sounding a little solemn:

"Thank you, and it was interesting to have meet you."

"You mean 'to have MET you'," said Ia.

Then they went up to the helicopter. Marcus was the last one to leave the cave. He stood and watched the others climbing the few yards up to the helicopter landing spot. He suddenly seemed to think of something. He watched Mina disappear over the edge but stayed where he was.

There was something he still had to do. He had forgotten something. Or rather: they had *all* forgotten something.

Right next to the wolves' cave was another cave. It was the third cave on Three Cave Mountain. And suddenly Marcus made up his mind. He wanted to know. He didn't want to leave Three Cave Mountain without having seen the third cave.

It was no more than fifty yards away. He had to go there.

There was a little path that ran parallel to the top of the mountain, and when he reached the third cave,

he thought at first that it was exactly like the second
one. A round opening, maybe five feet high. Perfectly
round. Cautiously he approached and looked inside the
cave.

At first he didn't see anything. The light was dim
inside the cave. Then he saw it. There was something
inside, something very big and brown. A very big creature was lying inside there, maybe asleep. But then he
saw the creature slowly lift his head and look at him.

It was a bear.

It was the same bear he had seen before, the one that had gone past the first cave and bellowed so that Mischa understood, the one that had warned them about the hunters. It was the same bear. Marcus had found the bear's den.

They looked at each other for a moment. Neither of them moved. Then Marcus said:

"Everything's cool now. The hunters are going to be caught soon. The other police helicopter is on its way. Those murderers won't be coming back."

The bear lay perfectly still, with only his head raised. Then he yawned, opening his gigantic mouth and shutting it again. Then he burrowed his head between his paws.

He wanted to sleep. It was if he wanted to say: Try and understand. But thanks anyway.

And then Marcus went back to join the others.

The helicopter with all its passengers slowly lifted off from Three Cave Mountain and swung eastward, heading for the hospital in Karlstad.

"Where did you go, Marcus?" said Ia, sounding a little annoyed. "What were you doing?"

"I saw a bear," said Marcus.

And then they all started laughing, as if from relief. It sounded like an explosion. The expedition was over, they had been in the dire need, but they had made it through, and they were laughing because they thought Marcus was so funny.

The only one not laughing was Marcus.

Grandpa lay on the stretcher, right next to the helicopter's window, and when the helicopter lifted off, he looked down at the mountain. The cloud was still hovering around the mountain, and the peak rose up like a big black elephant above all that whiteness, and at the very top were the two caves, and their entrances were like eyes looking back at him. The helicopter rose slowly. And then, all of a sudden, Grandpa saw something moving in the mouth of the third cave. He turned his head to see better and wiped off some moisture from the window.

And then he saw it very clearly.

A bear had come out of the cave, a gigantic brown bear who stood up on his hind legs and looked up at the helicopter.

A bear. Marcus had actually seen a real bear.

Then the helicopter picked up speed, the mountain grew smaller and smaller, and their course took them toward the east.

Grandpa turned to Marcus and asked him:

"Marcus, what did you say you saw?"

Marcus was still grumpy so he just said in a low voice:

"Well, I guess nobody believes me."

Then Grandpa gave him a long look and smiled a bit as he patted his head and said:

"Oh yes, Marcus. I believe you."

By then the helicopter was high up flying faster. They could no longer see Three Cave Mountain. The expedition had come to an end.

3.

The police caught the wolf murderers that very same night, first the one who had hurt himself, then the other one.

They had a van parked at the Community Center in Helgeboda, the one near Janne Johansson's farm, and the van was full of endangered birds they had shot, and stolen eggs. They were from Hannover, which is in Germany.

It wasn't clear whether they actually understood what Marcus had shouted at them. But it didn't matter.

He did shout. And they fled.

There was a huge amount of commotion after that.

Grandpa had his leg put in a cast at the university hospital in Karlstad, and he stayed there for a few days until he was allowed to go back to their house near Helgeboda. It was just as well that he had a few days of peace and quiet. It wasn't so easy to explain what the purpose of the whole expedition had been. When they heard about it, Mina and Moa's mother and father went nuts, and Marcus and Ia's parents did too, and everybody came up to Värmland. Gunilla had to put her foot down to keep them all from going to the hospital in Karlstad to yell at Grandpa.

What was he thinking, dragging the kids into such a mess?! Was he out of his mind?! Things could have gone terribly wrong!

But since the kids all looked quite lively and calm and thought the whole thing had been so exciting, the parents began to settle down. And Marcus's father, whose name was Mats, decided that he would buy an electric wheelchair for Grandpa. It was called a Handubischi and had three wheels, with a top speed of twelve miles an hour. But, as Marcus's father was very careful to report, it could be souped up to go twenty-five miles an hour. Grandpa sat down in the wheelchair, and then Mats realized that it could be used as a racing car.

They could ride around outside the house and around some posts that were set up on the lawn. Then they had a racetrack, and they could time the laps. First Grandpa drove a few laps, and his best time was one minute and forty-six seconds. Then they put him on the lawn with his leg in the cast stretched out straight in front of him, and Marcus was allowed to drive. He started out cautiously, and his first lap was one minute and thirty-two seconds, but then he picked up speed and overturned at the tight curve.

"Marcus," said his father. "Try and understand. You can't take that tight curve at top speed. You have to put on the brakes before you hit that turn. Let me show you. Here's the stopwatch. Now pay attention so you'll learn."

Grandpa sat on the lawn with his leg stretched out in front and watched. Next to him sat Mina, who was scratching the little puppy, the one named Elsa Gilbertsson.

"Do you remember how it all started?" asked Grandpa. "You were bitten by a crocodile and met those cannibals in the Congo. Wasn't that it?"

"Oh," said Mina, "I was just dreaming, you know."

"Are you sure?" asked Grandpa.

"Well, yes. I was so little back then. That was a long time ago."

Grandpa looked at her for a moment without saying anything. Out on the racetrack was Mats, who was Grandpa's son, and that meant he was a lot like him—just as childish, as Mats's wife Ingrid liked to say. Mats was approaching the tight curve and had decided to set a track record. He took the curve at top speed and with a crash turned over, rolled around, and then slid down the slope, right into a thicket of nettles. They heard a faint howl. Marcus glanced at his stopwatch with a bright smile but didn't switch it off. He looked happy.

"Yes," said Grandpa, "that was a long time ago. At least three weeks."

But Mina wasn't paying attention. She was sitting with her back to the racetrack, looking up at the forest, which no longer seemed menacing or dangerous to her. She closed her eyes and imagined herself going straight through the forest, along the route to base camp number one in the first cave, up the mountainside, and up to the other caves, the second and the third. She thought about the bear that she knew was sleeping soundly in the third cave. And she thought about the wolf mamma in the second cave, but most of all she thought about the wolf cub.

She was almost positive what little Maja-Rubert was doing right now.

The cub was probably sitting outside the cave and looking across the valley and the forest. Maybe she saw the smoke coming from the house in the distance, and a strip of Lake Vällen, and far beyond the lake the mountains of Norway. And the cub was no longer scared. She was probably thinking about Mina. She was probably thinking about what had happened and how she had been saved by a dog named Mischa and all the kids, and how she had slept inside a house. And Mina was positive that the wolf cub was longing for her terribly.

So that's that. That's what happened. That's the whole story.

ABOUT THE AUTHOR

PER OLOV ENQUIST is one of Sweden's most acclaimed writers—a novelist, playwright, and poet with works published in more than twenty-five countries. His novels include *The Royal Physician's Visit* (*New York Times* notable book, winner of Sweden's August Prize, France's *Prix du Meilleur Livre Étranger*, and the *Independent* Foreign Fiction Prize) and, most recently, *Lewi's Journey*.

ABOUT THE TRANSLATOR

TIINA NUNNALLY has received numerous awards for her translations, among them the Lewis Galantiére Prize of the American Translators Association and the PEN/Book-of-the-Month Club Translation Prize.

ABOUT THE ILLUSTRATOR

STINA WIRSEN is the head of the illustration department at Sweden's largest newspaper, a renowned fashion designer, and children's book illustrator. She is the recipient of the Elsa Beskow Award, Sweden's top prize of children's illustrators.

Noa

Maja Rubert

Mina

Morfar

Elsa

Skutt-en